Last Stories

WILLIAM TREVOR

VIKING
an imprint of
PENGUIN BOOKS

VIKING

UK | USA | Canada | Ireland | Australia
India | New Zealand | South Africa

Viking is part of the Penguin Random House group of companies
whose addresses can be found at global.penguinrandomhouse.com.

First published 2018

002

Copyright © The Estate of William Trevor, 2018

Set in 13.5/16 pt Garamond MT Std
Typeset by Jouve (UK), Milton Keynes

Printed and bound in Great Britain by Clays Ltd, Elcograf S.p.A.

A CIP catalogue record for this book is available from the British Library

HARDBACK ISBN: 978–0–241–33776–9
TRADE PAPERBACK ISBN: 978–0–241–33777–6

www.greenpenguin.co.uk

Contents

The Piano Teacher's Pupil

'The Brahms?' she said. 'Shall we struggle through the Brahms?'

The boy, whose first lesson with Miss Nightingale this was, said nothing. But gazing at the silent metronome, he smiled a little, as if the silence pleased him. Then his fingers touched the piano keys and when the first notes sounded Miss Nightingale knew that she was in the presence of genius.

* * *

Now in her early fifties, slender, softly spoken, with a quiet beauty continuing to distinguish her features, Miss Elizabeth Nightingale considered that she was fortunate in her life. She had inherited a house on the death of her father, and managed without skimping on what she earned as a piano teacher. She had known the passion of love.

She might have married, but circumstances had not permitted that: for sixteen years she had been visited instead by a man she believed would one day free himself from a wife he was indifferent to. That hadn't happened, and when the love affair fell apart there had been painful regret on Miss Nightingale's side; but since then she had borne her lover no ill will, for after all there was the memory of a happiness.

Miss Nightingale's father, a *chocolatier*, being widowed at the time of her birth, had brought his daughter up on his own. They became companions and remained so until his death, although he'd never been aware of the love affair that had been conducted for so long during his daily absences from the house. That love and her father's devotion were recollections that cheered Miss Nightingale's present solitude and somehow gave a shape to her life. But the excitement she experienced when her new pupil played for her belonged to the present, was fresh and new and intense: not ever before had she sensed genius in a child.

'Just a little fast.' She made her comment when the piece she had suggested came to an end. 'And remember the pianissimo.' She touched the music with the point of her pencil, indicating where she meant.

The boy did not respond, but smiled as he had before. His dark hair, not cut too short, was in a fringe. The skin of his face was delicate, unblemished, as pale as paper. There was a badge on the breast pocket of his blazer, a long-beaked bird feeding its young. The blazer was navy blue, the badge red, all of it rather ugly in Miss Nightingale's opinion.

'You'll practise it just a little slower, won't you?' she said.

She watched the boy reaching for the sheet on the music stand, standing up to do so. He dropped it into his music case.

'Friday again?' she said, standing up herself. 'Same time?'

With eagerness that might have been purely polite but which she sensed was not, he nodded. His shyness was a pleasure, quite unlike the endless rattling on of her more tiresome pupils. He'd had several music teachers before, his mother had said, rattling on herself, so fast it was hard to understand why he'd been moved from one to another. In a professional way Miss Nightingale had enquired about that, but nothing had been forthcoming.

She led the way from the room and handed the boy his cap from the hall-stand ledge, the same emblem of a bird on it. She stood for a moment by the open door, watching him close the gate behind him. His short trousers made her wonder if he was cold, his knees seeming vulnerable and fragile above grey woollen socks, the blue-and-red of his blazer and his cap repeated on the border. He waved and she waved back.

No other child was due that evening and Miss Nightingale was glad. She tidied her sitting room, reclaiming it after the week's visitors, her own again until ten o'clock on Monday morning when dull Francine Morphew came. Piano and sofa and armchairs crowded what space the room offered. Staffordshire figures of soldiers paraded on either side of a carriage clock on the mantelpiece. Pot lids and the framed trays of chocolate moulds her father had collected decorated the walls, among watercolours and photographs. Daffodils in vases were on the sofa table and on the corner shelf near the door.

When she had tidied, Miss Nightingale poured herself a glass of sherry. She would say nothing to the mother if the mother telephoned to ask how the boy was getting on. It was a secret to share with no one except the boy himself, to be taken for granted between them, not gone on about. The mother was a foolish kind of woman.

When Miss Nightingale had sat a little longer, she turned on the electric fire, for the April evening was chilly now. Warmly, happily, it seemed that years of encouragement and instruction – offered for the most part to children without talent or interest – had at last been rewarded. Within this small boy, so modest in his manner, there were symphonies unwritten, suites and concertos and oratorios. She could tell; she didn't even have to think.

While darkness gathered, and when her second glass of sherry had been sipped away almost to nothing, Miss Nightingale sat for a few minutes longer. All her life, she often thought, was in this room, where her father had cosseted her in infancy, where he had seen her through the storms of adolescence, to which every evening he had brought back from his kitchens another chocolate he had invented for her. It was here that her lover had pressed himself upon her and whispered that she was beautiful, swearing he could not live without her. And now, in this same room, a marvel had occurred.

She felt her way through the gloom to the light switch by the door. Enriched with echoes and with memories, the room would surely also be affected by this afternoon. How could it be the same?

But when Miss Nightingale turned on the light nothing had altered. It was only when she was drawing the curtains that she noticed there was a difference. The little snuff-box with someone else's coat of arms on it was missing from the window table.

* * *

The next Friday a porcelain swan went, and then the pot lid with a scene from *Great Expectations* on it, and then an earring she'd taken out because the clasp was faulty. A scarf, too flimsy to be of use to a boy, was no longer on its hall-stand peg when she looked for it one Saturday morning. Two of the Staffordshire soldiers went.

She didn't know how he did it. She watched, and saw nothing. She said nothing either, and so unaffected was the boy himself by what was happening,

so unperturbed by his own behaviour, that she began
to wonder if she could be mistaken, if it could be one
of her less attractive pupils who was light-fingered; or
even if she had only just noticed what might have been
taken from her over a period of time. But none of this
made sense and her flimsy excuses all fell apart. The
rose-petal paperweight was there when he began to
play his Chopin preludes. It was gone when she returned
from seeing him out.

She wasn't a teacher when she was with him because
there was so little for her to teach, and yet she knew
he valued her presence, that her being an audience of
one meant more to him than the comments she contributed. Could it be, she even wondered, that he helped
himself to what he thought of as a fee for his perform-
ance? Such childish fantasies were not unusual: she had
herself been given to make-believe and pretending. But
that, too, she dismissed, sensing it not to be true.

At night she lay awake, her distress and her bewilderment afterwards mercilessly feeding vivid dreams.
In them the boy was unhappy and she wanted to comfort him, to make him talk to her when he had finished
playing his pieces. In endless repetition she tried to say
that once she had taken a chocolate from her father's
special box, but she couldn't; and when, awake again,
she lay there in the dark she found herself a prey to
thoughts she'd never had before. She wondered if her
father had been all he had seemed, if the man she had

admired and loved for so long had made use of her affections. Had her father's chocolates been an inducement to remain with him in his house, a selfishness dressed up? Had the man who'd deceived his wife deceived his mistress too, since deception was a part of him, lies scattered through the passion that there was?

In the dark she pushed all that away, not knowing where it came from, or why it seemed to belong with what was happening now; but always it came back, as if a truth she did not understand were casting its light over shadows that had beguiled her once. Was theft nothing much, the objects taken so small, and plenty left behind? If she spoke, her pupil would not come again, even if she said at once that she forgave so slight a misdemeanour. Knowing so little, at least she was certain of that, and often did not look to see what was no longer there.

The spring of that year gave way to summer, a heatwave of parched days that went on until the rains of October. All that time, on Friday afternoons, the doorbell rang and he was there, the same silent boy who left his cap on the hall-stand ledge, who sat down at her piano and took her with him into paradise.

*   *   *

Miss Nightingale's other pupils came and went also, but among them only the boy never requested a different day, a different time. No note was ever brought by him, no excuse ever trotted out, no nuisance unrecognized for what it was. Graham talked about his pets to delay his unpractised piece. Diana wept, Corin's finger hurt, Angela gave up. Then smoothly in the run of time another Friday came, to take its place as the halcyon afternoon at the centre of Miss Nightingale's life. Yet each time after the boy left there was mockery in the music that faintly lingered.

*　*　*

The seasons changed again, and then again until, one day, the boy did not return. He had outgrown these music lessons and his school, and now was somewhere else.

For Miss Nightingale, his absence brought calm; and time passing further quietened her unease. If a lonely father had been a calculating man it mattered less now than it had when the thought was raw. If a beloved lover had belittled love it mattered less in that same soothing retrospect. She had been the victim, too, of the boy who had shown off to her his other skill. She had been the victim of herself, of her careless credulity, her wanting to believe what seemed to be. All that, she sensed, was true. Yet something still nagged. It seemed a right almost that she should understand a little more.

*　*　*

Long afterwards, the boy came back – coarser, taller, rougher in ungainly adolescence. He did not come to return her property, but walked straight in and sat down and played for her. The mystery there was in the music was in his smile when he finished, while he waited for her approval. And looking at him, Miss Nightingale realized what she had not before: that mystery was a marvel in itself. She had no rights in this. She had sought too much in trying to understand how human frailty connected with love or with the beauty that the gifted brought. There was a balance struck: it was enough.

The Crippled Man

'Well, there's that if you'd want it,' the crippled man said. 'It's a long time waiting for attention. You'd need tend the mortar.'

The two men who had come to the farmhouse consulted one another, not saying anything, only nodding and gesturing. Then they gave a price for painting the outside walls of the house and the crippled man said it was too much. He quoted a lesser figure, saying that had been the cost the last time. The men who had come looking for work said nothing. The tall one hitched up his trousers.

'We'll split the difference if that's the way of it,' the crippled man said.

Still not speaking, the two men shook their heads.

'Be off with you in that case,' the crippled man said.

They didn't go, as if they hadn't understood. It was a ploy of theirs to pretend not to understand, to frown and simulate confusion because, in any conversation, it was convenient sometimes to appear to be at a loss.

'Two coats we're talking about?' the crippled man enquired.

The tall man said they were. He was older than his

companion, grey coming into his hair, but that was premature: both were still young, in their twenties.

'Will we split the difference?' the crippled man suggested again. 'Two coats and we'll split it?'

The younger of the men, who had a round, moon face and wire-rimmed glasses, offered another figure. He stared down at the grey, badly cracked flags of the kitchen floor, waiting for a response. The tall man, whose arms hung loosely and lanky like his body, sucked at his teeth, which was a way he had. If it was nineteen years since the house had been painted, he said, the price would have been less than would be worthwhile for them now. Nineteen years was what they had been told.

'Are ye Polish?' the crippled man asked.

They said they were. Sometimes they said that, sometimes they didn't, depending on what they had previously ascertained about the presence of other Polish people in a locality. They were brothers, although they didn't look like brothers. They were not Polish.

A black cat crept about the kitchen, looking for insects or mice. Occasionally it would pounce on a piece of bark that had fallen off the firewood, or a shadow. Fourteen days the painting would take, the younger man said, and they'd work on a Sunday; then the cost of the work surfaced again. A price was agreed.

'Notes,' the tall man said, rubbing a thumb and forefinger together. 'Cash.'

And that was agreed also.

* * *

Martina drove slowly, as she always did driving back from Carragh. More than once on this journey the old Dodge had stopped and she had had to walk to Kirpatrick's Garage to get assistance. Each time the same mechanic told her the car belonged to the antique brigade and should have been off the road for the last forty years. But the ancient Dodge was part of Martina's circumstances, to be tolerated because it was necessary. And, driven slowly, more often than not it got you there.

Costigan had slipped in a couple of streaky instead of back rashers, making up the half-pound, he'd said, although he'd charged for back. She hadn't said anything; she never did with Costigan. 'Come out to the shed till we'll see,' he used to say himself, and she'd go with him to pick out a frozen pork-steak or drumsticks she liked the look of in the shed where the deep-freeze was, his hands all over her. He no longer invited her to accompany him to the deep-freeze, but the days when he used to were always there between them and she never ate pork-steak or chicken legs without being reminded of how afterwards he used to push the money back to her when she paid and how in the farmhouse she hid it in a Gold Flake tin.

She drove past the tinkers at the Cross, the children in their rags running about, feet bare, heads cropped. The woman whom the noise of the Dodge always brought out stared stonily, continuing to stand there when the car went on, a still image in the driving mirror. 'We'd do it for four and a half,' the man in Finnally's had offered when she'd asked the price of the electric cooker that was still in the window. Not a chance, she'd thought.

About to be fifty and putting on more weight than pleased her, Martina had once known what she wanted, but she wasn't so sure about that any more. Earlier in her life, a careless marriage had fallen apart, leaving her homeless. There had been no children although she had wanted them, and often since had thought that in spite of having to support them she might have done better if children had been there to make a centre for her life.

She drove through the turf bogs, a Bord na Móna machine drawn up at the cuttings, an uncoupled trailer clamped so that it would stay where it was. Nothing was going on, nothing had changed at the cuttings for maybe as long as nine months. The lack of activity was lowering, she considered every time she saw, yet again, the place as it had been the last time.

She turned at Laughil, the road darkened by the trees that overhung it. She couldn't remember when it was that she'd last met another car on this journey. She didn't try to. It didn't matter.

* * *

The two men drove away, pleased that they'd found work, talking about the man who'd called out and said come in when they'd knocked on the door. All the time they were there he had remained in his chair by the fire of the range, and when the price was agreed he'd said go to the scullery and get the whiskey bottle. He had gestured impatiently when they didn't understand, lifting his fist to his mouth, tossing back his head, the fist going with it, until they realized what he meant.

He was convivial then; and they noticed the glasses on the dresser and watched while he put them out on the table. They were uncertain only for a moment, then one of them unscrewed the cap on the bottle.

'We heard about Poland,' he said. 'A Catholic people. We'll drink to the work, will we?'

They poured more whiskey for him when he held out the glass. They had more themselves before they left.

* * *

'Who was here?'

Martina put the bag of groceries on the table as she spoke. The whiskey bottle was there, out of his reach, two empty glasses beside it, his own, empty also, in his hand. He held it out, his way of asking her to pour him more. He wouldn't stop now, she thought; he'd go on until the bottle was empty and then he'd ask if there was one unopened, and she'd say no, although there was.

'A blue van,' she said, giving him more drink, since there was no point in not.

'I wouldn't know what colour it was,' he said.

'A blue van was in the boreen.'

'Did you get the list?'

'I did.'

He'd had visitors, he said, as if the subject were a new one. 'Good boys, Martina.'

'Who?' she asked again.

He wanted the list back, and the receipt. With his stub of a pencil, kept specially for the purpose, he crossed off the items she took from the bags they were in. In the days when Costigan had been more lively she had enjoyed these moments of deception, the exact change put down on the table, what she had saved still secreted in her clothes until she could get upstairs to the Gold Flake tin.

'Polish lads,' he said. 'They'll paint the outside for us.' Two coats, he said, a fortnight it would take.

'Are you mad?'

'Good Catholic boys. We had a drink.'

She asked where the money was coming from and

he asked, in turn, what money she was talking about. That was a way he had, and a way of hers invariably to question any money's source: the subject, once raised, had a tendency to linger.

'What'd they take off you?' she asked.

With feigned patience, he explained he'd paid for the materials only. If the work was satisfactory he would pay what was owing when the job was finished.

Martina didn't comment on that. Angrily, she pulled open one of the dresser's two drawers, felt at the back of it and brought out a bundle of euro notes, fives and tens in separate rubber bands, twenties, fifties, a single hundred. She knew at once how much he had paid. She knew he would have asked the painters to reach in for the money since he couldn't himself. She knew they would have seen the amount that was left there.

'Why would they paint a house when all they have to do is walk in and help themselves?'

He shook his head. He said again the painters were fine Catholic boys. With patience still emphatic in his tone, he repeated that the work would be completed within a fortnight. It was the talk of the country, he said, the skills young Polish boys brought to Ireland. An act of God, he said. She wouldn't notice them about the place.

* * *

They bought the paint in Carragh, asking what would be best for the walls of a house. 'Masonry,' the man said, pointing at the word on a tin. 'Outside work, go for the masonry.'

They understood. They explained that they'd been given money in advance for materials and they paid the sum that was written down for them.

'Polish, are you?' the man enquired.

Their history was unusual. Born into a community of stateless survivors in the mountains of what had once been Carinthia, their natural language a dialect enlivened by words from a dozen others, they were regarded often now as gypsies. They remembered a wandering childhood of nameless places, an existence in tents and silent night-time crossings of borders, the unceasing search for somewhere better. They had separated from their family without regret when they were, they thought, thirteen and fourteen. Since then their lives were what they had become: knowing what to do, how best to do it, acquiring what had to be acquired, managing. Wherever they were, they circumvented what they did not call the system, since it was not a word they knew; but they knew what it meant and knew that straying into it, or their acceptance of it, however temporarily, would deprive them of their freedom. Survival was their immediate purpose, their hope that there might somewhere be a life that was more than they yet knew.

They bought brushes as well as the paint, and white spirit because the man said they'd need it, and filler because they'd been told the mortar required attention: they had never painted a house before, and didn't know what mortar was.

Their van was battered, pale blue patched up a bit with a darker shade, without tax or insurance although there was the usual evidence of both on the windscreen. They slept in the van, among the tools of one kind or another they had come by, with their mugs, plates, a basin, saucepan, frying pan, food.

In the dialect that was their language the older brother asked if they would spare the petrol to go to the ruins where they were engaged in making themselves a dwelling. The younger brother, driving, nodded and they went there.

*　*　*

In her bedroom Martina closed the lid of the Gold Flake tin and secured it with its rubber band. She stood back from the wardrobe looking-glass and critically surveyed herself, ashamed of how she'd let herself go, her bulk not quite obese but almost now, her pale blue eyes – once her most telling feature – half lost in folds of flesh. She had been still in her thirties when she'd first come to the farmhouse, still particular about how she looked and dressed. She wiped away the lipstick that had been smudged by

Costigan's rough embracing when for a few minutes she had been alone with him in the shop. She settled her underclothes where he had disturbed them. The smell of the shop – a medley of rashers, fly spray and the chickens Costigan roasted on a spit – had passed from his clothes to hers, years ago. 'Oh, just the shop,' she used to say when she was asked about it in the kitchen, but she didn't bother saying it any more.

They were distantly related, had been together in the farmhouse since his mother died twelve years ago and his father the following winter. It was another relative who had suggested the union, since Martina was on her own and only occasionally employed. Her cousin – for they had agreed that they were cousins of a kind – would have otherwise to be taken into a home; and she herself had little to lose by coming to a farm where the grazing was parcelled out, rent received annually, where now and again another field was sold. Martina's crippled cousin, who since birth had been confined as he was now, had for Martina the attraction of a legal stipulation: in time she would inherit what was left. Often people assumed that he had died. In Carragh they did, and people from round about who never came to the farmhouse did; talking to them, you could feel it. Martina didn't mention him herself except when the subject was brought up: there was nothing to say because there was nothing that had become different, nothing she could remark on.

He was asleep after the whiskey when she went downstairs and he slept until he was roused by the clatter of dishes and the frying of their six o'clock meal. She liked to keep him to time, to do what it said to do. She kept the alarm clock on the dresser wound, accurate to the minute by the wireless morning and evening. She collected, first thing, what eggs had been laid in the night. She got him to the kitchen from the back room as soon as she'd set the breakfast table. She made the two beds when he had his breakfast in him and she had washed up the dishes. On a day she went to Carragh she left the house at quarter past two; she'd got into the way of that. Usually he was asleep by the range then, as most of the time he was unless he'd begun to argue. If he had, it could go on all day.

'The Poles would be a nuisance about the place.' She had to raise her voice because the liver on the pan was spitting. The slightest sound – of dishes or cooking, the lid of the kettle rattling – and he said he couldn't hear her when she spoke. But she knew he could.

He said he couldn't now and she ignored him. He said he'd have another drink and she ignored that too.

'They're never a nuisance,' he said. 'Lads like that.'

He said they were clean, you'd look at them and know. He said they'd be company for her.

'One month to the next you hardly see another face, Martina. Sure, I'm aware of that, girl. Don't I know it the whole time.'

She cracked the first egg into the pool of fat she'd made by tilting the pan. She could crack open an egg and empty it with one hand. Two each they had.

'It needs the paint,' he said.

She didn't comment on that. She didn't say he couldn't know; how could he, since she didn't manage to get him out to the yard any more? She hadn't managed to for years.

'It does me good,' he said. 'The old drop of whiskey.'

She turned the wireless on and there was old-time music playing.

'That's terrible stuff,' he said.

Martina didn't comment on that either. When the slices of liver were black she scooped them off the pan and put them on their plates with the eggs. She got him to the table. He'd had whiskey enough, she said when he asked for more, and nothing further was said on the subject in the kitchen.

When they had eaten she got him to his bed, but an hour later he was shouting and she went to him. She thought it was a dream, but he said it was his legs. She gave him aspirins, and whiskey, because when he had both the pains would go. 'Come in and keep me warm,' he whispered, and she said no. She often wondered if the pains had maddened him, if his brain had been attacked, as so much else in his body was.

'Why'd they call you Martina?' he asked, still whispering. A man's name, he said; why would they?

'I told you the way of it.'
'You'd tell me many a thing.'
'Go to sleep now.'
'Are the grass rents in?'
'Go back to sleep.'

* * *

The painting commenced on a Tuesday because on the Monday there was ceaseless rain. The Tuesday was fine, full of sunshine, with a soft, drying breeze. The painters hired two ladders in Carragh and spent that day filling in where the stucco surface had broken away.

The woman of the house, whom they assumed to be the crippled man's wife, brought out soda scones and tea in the middle of the morning, and when she asked them what time was best for this – morning and afternoon – they pointed at eleven o'clock and half past three on the older brother's watch. She brought them biscuits with the tea at exactly half past three. She stayed talking to them, telling them where they could buy what they wanted in Carragh, asking them about themselves. Her smile was tired but she was patient with them when they didn't understand. She watched them while they worked and when they asked her what she thought she said they were as good as anyone. By the evening the repairs to the stucco had been completed.

Heavy rain was forecast for the Wednesday and it came in the middle of the afternoon, blown in from the west by an intimidating storm. The work could not be continued and the painters sat in their van, hoping for an improvement. Earlier, while they were working, there had been raised voices in the house, an altercation that occasionally gave way to silence before beginning again. The older painter, whose English was better than his brother's, reported that it had to do with money and the condition of the land. 'The pension is what I'm good for,' the crippled man repeatedly insisted. 'Amn't I here for the few bob I bring in?' The pension became the heart of what was so crossly talked about, how it was spent in ways it shouldn't be, how the crippled man didn't have it for himself. The painters lost interest, but the voices went on and could still be heard when one or other of them left the van to look at the sky.

Late in the afternoon they gave up waiting and drove into Carragh. They asked in the paint shop how long the bad weather would last and were advised that the outlook for several days was not good. They returned the ladders, reluctant to pay for their hire while they were unable to make use of them. It was a setback, but they were used to setbacks and, enquiring again in the paint shop, they learnt that a builder who'd been let down was taking on replacement labour at the conversion of a disused mill – an indoor site a few miles away. In the end the gaffer agreed to employ them on a day-to-day basis.

* * *

The rain affected the crippled man. When it rained he wouldn't stop, since she was confined herself, and when they had worn out the subject of the pension he would begin again about the saint she was named after. 'Tell me.' He would repeat his most regular request, and if it was the evening and he was fuddled with drink she wouldn't answer, but in the daytime he would wheedle, and every minute would drag more sluggishly than minutes had before.

He did so on the morning the painters took down their ladders and went away. She was shaking the clinkers out of the range so the fire would glow. She was kneeling down in front of him and she could feel him examining her the way he often did. You'd be the better for it, he said when she'd tell about her saint, and you'd feel the consolation of a holiness. 'Tell me,' he said.

She took the ash pan out to the yard, not saying anything before she went. The rain soaked her shoulders and dribbled over her face and neck, drenching her arms and the grey-black material of her dress, running down between her breasts. When she returned to the kitchen she did as he wished, telling him what he knew: that holy milk, not blood, had flowed in the body of St

Martina of Rome, that Pope Urban had built a church in her honour and had composed the hymns used in her office in the Roman breviary, that she had perished by the sword.

He complimented her when she finished speaking, while she still stood behind him, not wanting to look at him. The rain she had brought in with her dripped on to the broken flags of the floor.

* * *

The painters worked at the mill conversion for longer than they might have, even though the finer weather had come. The money was better and there was talk of more employment in the future; in all, nine days passed before they returned to the farmhouse.

They arrived early, keeping their voices down and working quickly to make up for lost time, nervous in case there was a complaint about their not returning sooner. By eight o'clock the undercoat was on most of the front wall.

The place was quiet and remained so, but wisps of smoke were coming from one of the chimneys, which the painters remembered from the day and a half they'd spent there before. The car was there, its length too much for the shed it was in, its rear protruding, and they remembered that too. Still working at the front of the house, they listened for footsteps in the yard, expecting the tea that before had come in the morning, but no tea came. In the afternoon, when the older brother went to the van for a change of brushes, the tea tray was on the bonnet and he carried it to where the ladders were.

In the days that followed this became a pattern. The stillness the place had acquired was not broken by the sound of a radio playing or voices. The tea came without additions and at varying times, as if the arrangement about eleven o'clock and half past three had been forgotten. When the ladders were moved into the yard the tray was left on the stop of a door at the side of the house.

Sometimes, not often, glancing into the house, the painters caught a glimpse of the woman whom they assumed to be the wife of the crippled man they had drunk whiskey with, who had shaken hands with both of them when the agreement about the painting was made. At first they wondered if the woman they saw was someone else, even though she was similarly dressed. They talked about that, bewildered by the strangeness they had returned to, wondering if in this country so abrupt a transformation was usual and often to be found.

Once, through the grimy panes of an upstairs window, the younger brother saw the woman crouched over a dressing-table, her head on her arms as if she slept, or wept. She looked up while he still watched, his curiosity beyond restraint, and her eyes stared back at him but she did not avert her gaze.

That same day, just before the painters finished their work, while they were scraping the last of the old paint from the kitchen window-frames, they saw that the crippled man was not in his chair by the range and realized that since they had returned after the rain they had not heard his voice.

* * *

Martina washed up their two cups and saucers, tea-spoons with a residue of sugar on them because they'd been dipped into the bowl when they were wet with tea. She wiped the tray and dried it, and hung the damp tea-towel on the line in the scullery. She didn't want to think, even to know that they were there, that they had come. She didn't want to see them, as all day yesterday she had managed not to. She hung the cups up and put the saucers with the others, the sugar bowl in the cupboard under the sink.

The ladders clattered in the yard, pulled out of sight for the night in case they'd be a temptation for the tinkers. She couldn't hear talking and doubted there was any. A few evenings ago when they were leaving they had knocked on the back door and she hadn't answered.

She listened for footsteps coming to the door again

but none came. She heard the van being driven off. She heard the geese flying over, coming from the water at Dole: this was their time. Once the van had returned when something had been left behind and she'd been collecting the evening eggs and had gone into the fields until it was driven off again. In the kitchen she waited for another quarter of an hour, watching the hands of the dresser clock. Then she let the air into the house, the front door and the back door open, as the kitchen windows were.

*　*　*

The dwelling they had made for themselves at the ruins was complete. They had used the fallen stones and the few timber beams that were in good condition, a doorframe that had survived. They'd bought sheets of old galvanized iron for the roof, and found girders on a tip. It wasn't bad, they said to one another; in other places they'd known worse.

In the dark of the evening they talked about the crippled man, concerned – and worried as their conversation advanced – since the understanding about payment for the painting had been made with him and it could easily be that when the work was finished the woman would say she knew nothing about what had been agreed, that the sum they claimed as due to them was excessive. They wondered if the crippled man had been taken from the house, if he was in a home. They wondered why the woman still wasn't as she'd been at first.

*   *   *

She backed the Dodge into the middle of the yard, opened the right-hand back door and left the engine running while she carried out the egg trays from the house and settled them one on top of another on the floor, all this as it always was on a Thursday. Hurrying because she wanted to leave before the men came, she locked the house and banged the car door she'd left open. But the engine, idling nicely, stopped before she got into the driver's seat. And then the blue van was there.

They came towards her at once, the one with glasses making gestures she didn't understand at first, before she saw what he was on about. A rear tyre had lost some air; he appeared to be saying he would pump it up for her. She knew, she said; it would be all right. She dreaded what would happen now: the Dodge would let her down. But when she turned off the ignition and turned it on again, and tried the starter with the choke out, the engine fired at once.

'Good morning.' The older man had to bend at the car window, being so tall. 'Good morning,' he said again, when she wound the window down although she hadn't wanted to. She could hear the ladders going up. 'Excuse me,' the man who was delaying her said, and she let the car creep on, even though he was leaning on it.

'He's in another room,' she said. 'A room that's better for him.'

She didn't say she had eggs to deliver because they wouldn't understand. She didn't say when you got this old car going you didn't take chances with it because they wouldn't understand that either.

'He's quiet there,' she said.

She drove slowly out of the yard and she stalled the engine again.

*   *   *

The painters waited until they could no longer hear the car. Then they moved the ladders from one upstairs window to the next until they'd gone all the way round the house. They didn't speak, only glancing at one another now and again, conversing in that way. When they had finished they lit cigarettes. Almost three-quarters of the work was done: they talked about that, and calculated how much paint was left unused and how much they would receive back on it. They did no work yet.

The younger brother left the yard, passing through a gateway in which a gate was propped open by its own weight where a hinge had given way. The older man remained, looking about, opening shed doors and closing them again, listening in case the Dodge returned. He leant against one of the ladders, finishing his cigarette.

Cloudy to begin with, the sky had cleared. Bright sunlight caught the younger brother's spectacles as he came round the side of the house, causing him to take them off and wipe them clean as he passed back through the gateway. His reconnoitre had led him through a vegetable patch given up to weeds, into what had been a garden, its single remaining flower-bed marked with seed packets that told what its several rows contained. Returning to the yard, he had kept as close to the walls of the house as he could, pressing himself against the stucco surface each time he came to a window, more cautious than he guessed he had to be. The downstairs rooms revealed no more than those above them had, and when he listened he heard nothing. No dogs were kept. Cats watched him without interest.

In the yard he shook his head, dismissing his fruitless efforts. There was a paddock with sun on it, he said, and they sat there munching their stale sandwiches and drinking a tin of Pepsi Cola each.

'The crippled man is dead.' The older brother spoke softly and in English, nodding an affirmation of each word, as if to make his meaning clear in case it was not.

'The woman is frightened.' He nodded that into place also.

These conjectures were neither contradicted nor commented upon. In silence the two remained in the sun and then they walked through the fields that neglect had impoverished, and in the garden. They looked down at the solitary flowerbed, at the brightly coloured seed packets marking the empty rows, each packet pierced with a stick. They did not say this was a grave, or remark on how the rank grass, in a wide straight path from the gate, had been crushed and recovered. They did not draw a finger through the earth in search of seeds where seeds should be, where flowers were promised.

'She wears no ring.' The older brother shrugged away that detail, depriving it of any interest it might have had, irrelevant now.

Again they listened for the chug of the car's unreliable engine but it did not come. Since the painting had made it necessary for the windows to be eased in their sashes, any one of them now permitted entry to the house. This was not taken advantage of, as yesterday it would have been, this morning too. Instead, without discussion, the painting began again.

Undisturbed, they worked until the light went. 'She will be here tomorrow,' the older brother said. 'She will have found the courage, and know we are no threat.'

In the van on the way back to their dwelling they talked again about the woman who was not as she had been, and the man who was not there. They guessed and wondered, supposed, surmised. They cooked their food and ate it in uncomfortable confinement, the shreds and crumbs of unreality giving the evening shape. Neither impatience nor anger had allowed a woman who had waited too long to wait again, until she was alone: they sensed enough of truth in that. They smoked slow cigarettes, instinct directing through. The woman's history was not theirs to know, even though they were now part of it themselves. Their circumstances made them that, as hers made her what she had become. She held the whip hand because it was there for her to seize. She'd see to it that still the pension came. No one would miss the crippled man, no one visited a lonely place. Tomorrow the woman would pay for the painting of the house. Tomorrow they would travel on.

At the Caffè Daria

Along a single wall of the Caffè Daria the scarlet upholstered banquettes haven't changed, the ornate brass foot-rail at the counter remains. The mural flower patterns have yet again been renewed in the same pastel shades, the tables are still not set too close together. The floor, although it's tiled, still does not echo footsteps.

Often crowded, noisy with chatter, the caffè is quiet in the early morning. Business people hurry in then, for the breakfast that was forgone in earlier-morning haste. The first of the shoppers come later, on their way from the suburbs to the exhausting bustle of the streets. Friends meet then, regulars reach for the newspapers on their wooden hangers.

The croissants are famous. The lunchtime scrambled eggs with smoked salmon is said to be the best in London, the coffee is never less than it should be. The little apple tarts are a recent speciality, the *tarte au citron* is borrowed from the French.

The caffè has a story. In 1949 Andrea Cavalli sold the family vineyards he had inherited before the war and left Piedmont, and Italy, for ever. He was not embittered, even when the wife he still loved was taken from him by a poet who dedicated to her all he subsequently composed. Desolate and alone, Andrea Cavalli travelled the shattered countries of a Europe that reflected his melancholy, a Europe that would never be the same again. Nor, he knew, would he. He took with him on his lonely wanderings a woman's countenance he knew he would never in reality see again, a voice that softly echoed even while he slept, a desire that would not go away. How dull he was, he thought, knowing only the clay of estates that were no longer his, and the ripening of grapes. The poet, whom he had never met, he imagined: a careless, handsome fellow whom no woman could be blamed for loving. As he travelled, Andrea Cavalli knew that he could never challenge the skilful rhyming of words, or clever thoughts.

Without a destination as he went on, the cruel land-scape of devastation ever grimmer, he found himself finally wandering the broken streets of London. Such was the lowness of his spirits that he was seized, in desperation, with an eccentricity: to do something to confirm his existence, an unknown man in a country strange to him, to offer it what he could, since it had so little itself. That he was rich was his only power: among London's bomb sites he created the Caffè Daria, immortalizing as he did so his lost wife. He honoured her because he wanted to, knowing that for him there could only ever be this gesture. It pleased him that he had found the courage to make it, that her name would always be there in this distant city, that nothing of what he'd done had been a mistake.

* * *

One morning long after the time of Andrea Cavalli, the slight figure of a quietly dressed woman in her middle age occupies in the Caffè Daria the table she particularly likes. The waitresses smile at her as they pass and she smiles too; the young Italian manager has greeted her warmly on her arrival. It may be that she has been coming to the Caffè Daria for longer than anyone else; she doesn't know, but it's not unlikely, for she remembers when she was five being here with her father, who was attracted by the caffè's stylishness. Years later – at a time for her of wretchedness and disappointment – that same stylishness was a solace, as other people's lives observed were. Her features now are slightly lined but her eyes are clear and even bright, her hair skilfully streaked, a grey pervasiveness kept at bay.

Once a dancer, she is a publisher's reader now and often brings to the caffè the typescripts she has been asked to comment on. She has come with two this morning, a medieval murder-mystery and a tale of passion set in the Australian outback. Neither enthrals her; in both the quality of the writing is poor, which

she records with professional politeness, while holding nothing back. She is touched sometimes, drawn
into what has been written, as she was when she read
only for pleasure. She did so hungrily and widely then,
and as perceptively as she now assesses promise or
achievement. No one has taught her that skill, but it is
there and makes a living for her.

She pours more coffee, all that's left in her cafetière,
then looks about her. A few of the faces at the other
tables are familiar, the banquettes too far away to
observe in any detail. Behind her somewhere a
couple edgily disagree, the timbre of their voices suggesting the beginning of a quarrel. She doesn't try to
listen; she would have once and often still does, here
or anywhere.

In the 1970s, before she knew what a publisher's
reader was, Anita Lyde, as she was then, danced with
the Fireflies, delighting in the excitement of being a
television song-and-dance girl. She was admired by
an older man with charm to burn, and handsome in
his way, who in time asked her if she could bear to
marry him. She meant it when she said she couldn't
bear not to.

A waitress brings more hot milk before she asks for
it. She opens the letters she picked up before she left
her flat but there is nothing of interest among them
and she puts them back in their envelopes to drop
into a waste-bin later. She doesn't mind being alone.

She did once but doesn't now, and supposes that being alone has become part of her, as her mornings in the Caffè Daria have too.

She gathers up her papers and reads again what she has written, makes changes, adds a little. 'Temporary interruption' is a clue in a crossword she earlier almost finished. *Pause*, she fills in now, *annulled* for 'Declared invalid'. A woman who has just come in hesitates at the door, appears to be about to go away, then changes her mind. A striking figure in well-cared-for middle age also, she makes her way through the tables. Watching her, Anita realizes she is Claire. The classic beauty passed on by a Danish mother – with sky-blue eyes and Scandinavian fairness – is still there. That protruding chairs are pulled back to allow her more room to pass, that occasionally a man stands up, that she is smiled at, are somehow reminders of Claire too. Anita's instinct is not to let herself be seen but she knows she has been.

They played with dolls once upon a time, Anita round-faced and trusting, Claire beautiful already. They shared their childhood fears, their knowledge as they came to know it, confessed their adolescent guilt. They giggled together at fat Miss Sumac of their boarding school and smoked the cigarettes the French girl gave them; they cut out photographs of Steve McQueen, collected the same good wishes in their autograph books. They danced together with the

Fireflies and it was then that the Caffè Daria became their most special place. Anita told the tale of Andrea Cavalli's consuming love, and both so admired his generosity that between them they transformed him into a figure of heroic awe. They touched the things he'd touched and called themselves ridiculous for doing so, and yet they did it. The Fireflies' reign as television's favourite dance group was over when Anita had her wedding party in the caffè's private room, but the Fireflies danced again, for one last time, that afternoon. Soon afterwards, so Anita has heard, Veronica tried to become a nun but they wouldn't have her. Eunice runs a dogs' hotel near Ashford. Dolly Olden married four times, Tilda lives in Weston-super-Mare. Alice went to Canada, Maisie became a beautician. And Claire is here.

'Why have you come?' Anita asks, and Claire for a moment seems not to know. Yet nothing else in her manner suggests that she is here today without a purpose. Her voice is empty of expression when she speaks. She looks away for an instant before she does.

'Just after four I sensed his stillness. I turned the light on and I saw.'

'Gervaise has died?'

Claire nods, is silent. How patronizing, Anita reflects, the smile that isn't there today once was, how treacherous the sky-blue eyes. How much she detested then the Scandinavian beauty and wished the perfect profile maimed, how often made the graceful walk a dragging slouch.

This bitterness, too long possessed, no longer shames Anita but has instead become a nourishment, her way out of managing disappointment. Politely she offers coffee, and indicates the table's only other chair.

'The house?' she asks, to use up time.

'The house will go. Since there are debts.'

They both have lived in it. Anita made it as she wanted it to be, Claire moved the furniture about and painted doors and windowsills a colour she preferred. She changed the lampshades, the wallpaper in the hall, replaced the knives and forks. Gervaise at thirty-four was Anita's older man when she came to his house as a bride of nineteen, artless and in love. A legacy made life easy for Gervaise. He lived as he wished to live: playing the cello, teaching himself Russian, buying the unfashionable paintings he admired. As well, he dabbled a bit with words, he used to say, but nothing much ever came of that. Tall, fair-haired, with sleepily amused eyes, he gambled modestly, the pleasures of racecourses attracting him as much as his unfashionable paintings did, or Proust or Stendhal.

'Death is not something for the telephone,' Claire says. 'I hoped you might be here. You are the first to be told.'

Anita watches her going as she has watched her

coming. They have not smiled in each other's company. At the door Claire does not look back.

*   *   *

Anita is less affected by her husband's death than she was by his saying they had made a mistake in marrying. With terrible tenderness he murmured it and then, regret becoming sympathy, offered his prediction: that for her one day there would be someone else too. There never was. She knew there couldn't be.

On a Sunday morning she left the house, his cello heard in an upstairs room, her suitcases in the hall, to be collected some other time. She did not say goodbye but simply walked away, to weep in silent Sunday streets, going nowhere, only wanting to be somewhere else. Why Claire? her single thought was. Why Claire, when Veronica or Tilda would have done, or any of the others? Why was she twice betrayed?

Canoes, she pencils in. 'Small boats for strange oceans' is the clue. *Losers* are the odd sorels who never win. 'Classical dance' is *ballet*. She puzzles over 'concentric circles that might be flower petals', gives up on 'ski turn' and then remembers *stem*.

Had he as he lay dying whispered her name and wondered whose it was? Had he known why it was Claire who smoothed his pillow, or in the blur of approaching death imagined it was the girl who was still his wife? Had he for one bright moment seen her as she was when she danced and sang? Had he remembered loving her and no one else? What were his thoughts while death reached out, or was there any thought at all?

*   *   *

It is a grey, high house on a corner, in a neighbourhood that had been fashionable but no longer is. Flats and short lets and the ground-floor businesses of mortgage advisers and debt-collectors have changed the character of a once-gracious street. Only the house on the corner is as the others in the past have been, a single dwelling, some of the rooms not often used. Its sole occupant now is Claire, her footsteps echoing in a hollow silence, for already the carpets have been taken up and much of the furniture sold. But Claire, as she goes from room to room, hears more: hushed whispers on the telephone are there again, charm-wrapped and secret. Deception is confessed: the attractions of an attractive man come at a price. In the house Claire bore all that Anita could not have. She bears it still and knows she always will.

His suits hang in the hall, waiting for the charity people to come. Shirts are laid out on a bedsheet on the floor, together with the stripes and dots of many ties. There is a row of polished shoes. On a recessed shelf in what has been the dining room are the carefully typed pages of a novel, begun but not continued with. On the shelf immediately beneath it a collection of objects has accumulated and been kept: a single jigsaw piece, a flattened coin, an inkwell lid, a marbled egg, seashells, a blue-painted stick, a miniature gyroscope, a flint, and things that are part of other things. Claire throws none away.

His bed was carried down to this room when he said he would prefer it and it was known that he would not walk about the house again. His being downstairs was more convenient for his visitors too, and many came. They brought him wine, confectionery for his sweet tooth, the magazines he liked. They dwindled to a handful, then did not come at all, agreeing that it was better so. He had maintained he was unworthy to be a father and so there were no children to stand around his deathbed, none now to mourn him with a family's special grief, to keep him for a while alive, as a family can. He called himself a remnant when he felt he had become one. But in his now forever quietened face his languid smile and the amusement in his eyes had still seemed to be there.

The avenue is long, she reads from the writing that is unfinished. *Trees meet overhead, their winter fall of leaves, damp now, cushioning his footsteps as he goes on. The stillness has a quality of its own; the sunshine that has lit the hedge poppies and meadow daisies is lost in the twilight of the trees. No rabbits burrow, no squirrels search; no voices echo. What sounds there are are of the trees.*

His family's place that once had been, and Claire searches for more about it but finds nothing. She gathers up race-cards and betting slips, begging letters, forgotten uncashed cheques, a passionate note in a woman's handwriting among them. This too she has not seen before, for he was considerate in his way and carelessness was foolish, so he said.

The house is cold. She finds an overcoat among the clothes that wait in the hall, one that's warmer than any of hers. In the kitchen, where she has mostly lived since so much of the furniture went, she pours herself a drink, adding vermouth to the ordinariness of gin. She lights the gas oven, leaving its door open to warm the air. She sits on the edge of the trestle bed she sleeps on here, her hands held out to the warmth, her glass on the floor beside her. She has always hated the cold.

* * *

Anita eats lightly in the evenings, often no more than soup and toast or an egg. For tonight she has bought slices of turkey breast and will not cook.

She didn't go to the funeral although Claire had sent a note: the day, the time. Instead she went to the cinema, to see a film she'd seen before. Walking to Baker Street, she imagined the mourners gathering, some old friend making the most of the oration, a generosity remembered, and niceness. All that was months ago and there was nothing special about the day, or even about Gervaise's dying, since he hadn't been part of her life for so long.

She slices tomato and cucumber for a salad, shakes together spinach and rocket, scatters olives. When she was first deserted she went back often to be near the house where so briefly she lived and was happy. She stood about where she could not be seen, peered through chinks in lit-up windows when it was dark, seeing nothing but still remaining. She drew back into deeper shadows when there were footsteps; she might well have worn a veil and wanted to, but that had seemed dramatic and unreal.

She mixes oil and vinegar. Her radio plays softly, music she likes but can't identify. She doesn't have television, had long ago decided that television was something for an audience of more than one, to be watched in company and talked about. She reads a typescript she hasn't finished with while she eats. She couldn't have managed the funeral, no one but Claire knowing who she was.

*   *   *

The death occurred when a July dawn was flickering into life. It is October when Claire finishes in the house. A 'For Sale' board is in place but no one comes to see the house, no interest has been shown in it. It's an awkward size, the agents say, too big, less easy to divide than other houses in this street; being on a corner isn't in its favour. Without its furniture, neglect is apparent in the rooms, dark areas on walls where wardrobes or tallboys have protected surfaces from the sun. Here and there, wallpaper hangs loose, plaster falls away.

Oppressed by her surroundings, Claire goes for walks, an activity that hasn't attracted her before. She finds the river and walks along the towpath in one direction or the other; she comes to know streets and districts she hasn't known before. Still mourning, lost in her loneliness, she often feels tired almost as soon as she sets out, then hurries back and time hangs heavily. There have been other friendships besides Anita's, but so entirely did she give herself to Gervaise that these have lapsed and she dreads attempting to renew them, not knowing why she does. One foggy November morning she makes her way again to the Caffè Daria.

* * *

Anita, that morning, arrives at the caffè later than usual and as she does is at once aware of someone intent on attracting her attention. A hand is raised as if to wave but quickly then is lowered, as if on second thoughts waving is inappropriate.

How wan she seems, Anita reflects, recognizing Claire, who despite her change of mind continues to look expectantly in Anita's direction. There is a hollowness about her face, Anita's thought goes on. It was not there before.

'Your cafetière?' a waitress greets her and Anita nods, gesturing at her usual table, emptily waiting for her. She pauses when she reaches Claire's.

'I thought I'd come,' Claire says.

Anita nods again, as if she understands why Claire is here, which she does not. In her slim black attaché case are the papers she needs for her morning's work, a newspaper too, the day's post. She smiles, feeling that she must. She can tell it's an effort for Claire to smile too, although she tries.

'Well,' Anita says, not making it a question. Noticing that the cafetière she ordered has been brought to her table, she might say she is pressed this morning and hurry off to it. She wonders why she doesn't, why she has paused here at all.

'An awful month,' Claire says. 'November.'

Her hair is lank, apparent now as it wasn't from a distance. Her make-up is carelessly applied.

Slowly Anita sits down, her slowness intended, denying a willingness to converse. The caffè isn't full and when she looks around people nod or smile, knowing her well yet not at all. It's a nice way to be known, Anita has often thought in the Caffè Daria.

'The house is bleak,' Claire says. 'My God, how bleak it is.'

The words mean something else, Anita knows, and imagines more: childless women as they are, they might turn to one another now. But pretence's truth is shoddy, without a heart. And the past is too far off, its laughter does not echo, its flimsy shadows fall away.

'I'm sorry,' Claire says, the useless words whispered as if they deserve no more than that.

'Why have you come?' Anita repeats her question of months ago, precise and cold, as it was then.

'Perhaps I've come to beg you to forgive me. You bear Gervaise's name and I do not. Gervaise has died and we and it are left.'

'But we are as we are, not as we were. Death exorcizes nothing. I was a passing fancy in a spoilt man's life and you were everything. It's that that's left.'

Anita stands up, and Claire does too. In silence she begs again, a pleading in her eyes.

'Gervaise did not know about being faithful,' she says before she goes. 'He never was. Nor was I everything.'

But Anita's unforgiving resolve does not weaken and the conversation ends in silence.

The lunchtime waiters come, passing through the caffè to have a coffee at the back. The empty tables are cleared, reservation cards put out on some. Anita arranges her papers, begins to make her notes.

* * *

The towpath is becoming familiar territory now, the sluggish traffic on the water, the stunted winter growth, the runners, the walkers. Are they curious, Claire wonders, about a solitary woman dressed more formally than they, a woman who was not here before and is so often now? She's unacknowledged by these more serious people of the towpath; there is no nod, no smile, no suggestion of affection, as there is for Anita in the Caffè Daria. Claire hurries when it's cold, as if she, too, is here for a purpose. One of a modest lunchtime crowd in the Marquis of Granby, she makes time pass when she reaches it, whisky warming her, the counter newspaper claimed. The December twilight is darkening when she walks back to the house, through streets alive with Christmas decorations. The news items she read earlier are repeated on the television. The house remains unsold.

When the 'For Sale' board first went up Anita often went to see if it was still there. She has done so since; it always is. She tells herself that casual curiosity is the reason for her returning to this quiet street; she knows it isn't. The house is where she was loved, where alone with Gervaise she was happier than ever she had been before or ever has been since. The house was hers as much as it was his, he used to say, for in its rooms they belonged to one another and promised they always would. 'You stay,' he said when they did not. 'I'll be the one to go away.' In her dreams she haunts the house. In her dreams it is still hers.

The winter of that year passes. Snow whitens London's parks, clings everywhere to what it can. Piled up, it turns to grey and then to slush. Spring comes as a relief. Anita's mornings at the Caffè Daria, discontinued during the worst of the weather, are resumed. Claire does not again appear there, and Anita supposes that she has at last come to terms with the death. In time she will find someone else, why should she not? Behind the quiet windows and the faded, trim front door she'll make a life again. Some other man will pay the debts, the house will not be sold.

But when a warm May has come and almost gone Anita sees that the red-and-blue 'For Sale' sign is still there, bright against the grey façade. She has always known that her skulking in this street is undignified and no doubt a source of comment. But still she comes, to pause for a moment, for a moment is enough, then to go on as other people do. One evening, quite late and dark already, she notices that the front door doesn't seem quite closed. It isn't when she tries it.

Her instinct is to walk away and she obeys it, telling herself when later she experiences pangs of doubt that a door left open in error, or for a purpose, is not unusual. Living there herself, she had often left her keys upstairs and when she was going no further than the shops had not trudged back up for them. But doubt is still not satisfied and she goes back.

No light shows in a window, the house's blankness making it seem another of those that are offices by day. Anita touches the door with the tips of her fingers and feels it yielding. Keys hanging in it rattle. She rings the bell. She pushes the door open when nothing happens.

Still, there's no sound of movement, no sudden glare of light. Could Claire have gone to bed, forgetting that she hadn't closed the door? But Claire in all her life has not been one to go to bed early, nor did she in the past often forget things. Anita waits in the unlit hall, wanting to go away and unable to make herself. She turns the stair lights on, remembering where the switch is. 'Claire,' she calls out, and there is no response.

In the kitchen there is a trestle bed, its sheets and blankets folded. An unwashed glass is on the table, bottles in a row beneath the sink. Food, not cooked, is wrapped in plastic, ready to be thrown away. Papers have been burnt, their feathery black embers in a firegrate. Unopened letters are in a pile.

Anita senses desperation in all this, a hurriedness in what's done and what is left. The thought comes from nowhere, but remains and then is more than first it was. Had there been desperation in the sunken features, the careless make-up and neglected hair? Had desperation ordered each unexpected return to the caffè, inspired the longing that was not articulated?

Again Anita wants to go away, to leave all this and whatever else there is. She saw the suffering, she knew that it was there. She punished, she didn't hesitate. She knows she didn't: it was her due.

Upstairs, in other rooms she turns on lights. Clothes fill a wardrobe that her own once did. She opens drawers and finds them empty. She reaches into shelves for what might be at the back. There is no handbag, no purse. There is no note: the open door said all there was to say.

What happens, Anita wonders, to people when they walk away? What then do they become? Their absence is a kind of death; is it death, too, for them? Or in some distant place can memory be closed down and guilt assuaged? She calls Claire's name again but still there's silence.

She turns the upstairs lights out and, descending to the hall, imagines Claire standing there, having just come in, her handbag that moment put down. The image is held when Anita pauses on a landing. She listens for a rustle, a footstep muffled, hardly there. She looks again in rooms in case she has overlooked one, or any sign that tells her something. She waits a little longer, then slowly continues on her way downstairs. In the hall she takes the keys out of the door she found open and turns out the last of the lights.

The street outside is quiet and she waits there too for the sound of footsteps coming. She goes away and then returns and waits again, the night becoming empty all around her. She locks the door and pushes the keys through the letter-box, and hears them clattering on the floor.

*　*　*

In the Caffè Daria there are new faces, and others that were often there no longer are. The older of the two coffee machines has been replaced; one Sunday the ceiling was repainted, the same light shade of blue.

At her usual table, Anita reads of violent crime and difficult love, of human frailty and of redemption, of anguish and its healing. Sometimes she looks up and there is Claire come back, to be Claire for another moment, until she's someone else. Anita's greeting, already enlivening her features, is put away and she is left to wonder and to wait. Claire is somewhere. If Anita prayed she would pray to know where. If she knew the secrets of telepathy she would employ them.

The sales board has been taken down. Other people live in the house. Claire cherishes in her lonely solitude what Anita, in hers, too late embraces now: all that there was before love came, when friendship was the better thing.

Taking Mr Ravenswood

Belonging to her time on the counters – before they moved her upstairs to Customer Care – Mr Ravenswood's easy smile stirred in Rosanne's memory, the paisley handkerchief tidily protruding from the top pocket of a softly checked jacket, the tweed hat on the counter for the duration of whatever transaction there was. Stylish in his manner, Mr Ravenswood was friendly in a way the other men who came to the counters never were, and always asked her how she was. The cheques he regularly lodged were dividends, unearned income from inherited means, and you could sense from his manner a faint disdain of money's self-importance.

On the screen in front of Rosanne a mass of further material gathered: Mr Ravenswood's address – 81 Radcliffe Square – hadn't changed in the years that had passed; the balance in the current account – as carelessly large as she remembered it had always been – at present stood at £44,681.29, with £300,050 in his deposit account. The current account had been a joint one in the past, when Mr Ravenswood's wife was alive, but that was before Rosanne knew him. Not that she did know Mr Ravenswood, not that she had ever thought of him like that. She'd been astonished when he invited her to have dinner with him.

He hadn't pressed her. He'd watched her hesitating, then had mentioned the name of a restaurant, and she said she didn't think she could. She changed her mind because she was on her own at the time and feeling low, Keith having packed his things after yet another quarrel. The Plume d'Or, the restaurant was called, in a street off Pall Mall. She had difficulty in finding it and felt awkward because she was late. But Mr Ravenswood shook his head and said the best people nearly always were.

*   *   *

The girls at the other desks were turning off their computers, a few already putting on their coats. 'You'll come to the corner, Rosie?' one of them invited, referring to the bar where, on Friday evenings or when it was someone's birthday, office workers gathered to celebrate for an hour or so. It was a birthday today, but Rosanne apologized, as so often she had to: there was her child to collect and she hadn't said she'd be late.

She turned off her own computer, and stayed a little longer in the quiet room. Downstairs, the security man let her out.

The streets were crowded with office workers going home; so was the Tube. Sometimes someone trying to get off with her offered Rosanne his seat, but not this evening. Sluggishly, her journey took her out of the city, into the hinterland that was hers and had been all her life. Kensal Green, Willesden Junction, Harlesden, Stonebridge Park, Wembley Central: she knew the stations too well, not even looking when another one was reached. Her thoughts were full of Keith, as she had known they would be, his pale, sharp features, sandy hair drooping over a narrow forehead, his crooked grin. 'You'll take this guy?' he'd said when, together again, she'd told him about her evening with Mr Ravenswood, the question casually asked, for Keith was good at that. The old guy had been whistled, he said when he heard more about the evening, of course he had. Stuff like that was what old guys got up to – getting whistled and getting girls whistled too, and afterwards nothing mentioned, nothing much remembered. Too late, Rosanne had realized she shouldn't have said anything. Her mother, who considered Keith unreliable, referred to him as the unnecessary complication in her daughter's life, at best a nuisance. Rosanne loved him.

She did not deny that complication came into it: that Keith was a complicated person she accepted as the truth because he said so himself, and because it was so often confirmed by his decisions, the conclusions he reached, and his capacity for making the most of unpromising circumstances. It was almost perfectly exemplified by what became, in time, his obsession with Mr Ravenswood, when Rosanne's stubborn resistance to suggestions of how they might take advantage of what Keith called a 'weakness for girls' strained the convoluted nature of their relationship. 'No, no, I couldn't,' she had since continued to protest. 'Not ever.'

Disagreement was fractious then, and bitter later. Why could she not? What was her trouble? When chance for once was offering so much, why couldn't she see sense, since so often she had before? Rosanne had no answer to that, for it was true. The little Shrewsbury table, hardly bigger than a doll's, lent to her by her mother, had not been theirs to sell yet she and Keith had sold it. The instruction as to how her father's bequest of his savings account should be spent was ignored. A handbag found on the floor by a café table was picked up by Keith to be handed in. Rosanne wondered if it had been but didn't ask.

She got a seat at Wembley Central and closed her eyes, Keith still there. He drove a van, delivering packages and parcels all over south-west London. He was in films, he said when he and Rosanne first met, on a Starbucks sofa one Saturday morning, and his claim was not entirely untrue: he'd once been a crowd-scene extra in a production that ran out of funds and was abandoned. He talked about the big-time, and when Rosanne accidentally became pregnant she allowed the baby to be born in the hope that this would bring him down to earth a bit, but it didn't. In the end it was her continuing reluctance in their long dispute about Mr Ravenswood that caused Keith to leave for longer than usual. 'You're a loser,' he'd said, his favourite comment on their relationship.

At the Underground station she picked up an *Evening Standard* and two packets of crisps, then walked in a gathering drizzle to Purse Street to collect her child from Nancy Pollitt, the child-minder whom she neither liked nor trusted. She felt drained by the day, although the day was not yet over. The walk took twenty minutes.

A van was drawn up at the post-box in Stanley Street, the driver collecting the handful of letters that had caught the late post. Sometimes he was there, or waiting in his van for time to pass. A notice in red, recently pasted, announced that from 1 September this last collection of the day would cease. 'Evening,' the van-driver said as Rosanne went by. Further on, although brightly lit, the Running Horse pub was silent. When it filled up later, people would complain about the noise.

Nancy Pollitt's front door opened after a delay, and then there was the usual grim greeting, without a smile, a suppressed sigh to indicate disapproval. The hall smelt of cigarette smoke and stale food. 'Fine,' Nancy Pollitt said when she was asked how the day had been. 'Fine.'

It was another walk of much the same length to

7A Tangar Street, where Rosanne lived, the entrance to her two-roomed flat in Tangar Passage. Her latch-key had to be adjusted in the lock it had been inadequately cut for, pressed down a little and not pushed too far in, all of which added irritation to Rosanne's tiredness and her renewed doubts about Nancy Pollitt's suitability as a child-minder.

In the hall, with one hand she folded the pushchair, holding her child, somnolent until now, in her other arm. She was not impatient and as best she could she soothed the crankiness that had begun. Upstairs, on what had been a landing until a chipboard partition had made it part of her accommodation, she mixed a jar of Turkey Casserole with Pure Vegetable and immersed the combination in a saucepan of boiling water. She warmed up the cod and mushroom bake from last night for herself, hoping it was all right, because you weren't meant to.

Going to bed, when she had watched television and read the *Evening Standard*, when the flat had warmed up a bit, she felt less dreary. Sometimes it wasn't bad, being alone, especially when she was tired it wasn't, no effort made, none necessary, and the silence when the television was turned off came as a balm. But the silence could be a vacuum too, and often felt like that.

Her phone rang when she was brushing her teeth and for a moment she thought it might be Keith because this was a time he used to ring. But someone asked her if she was the Gas, and she said she wasn't. She knew where to find Keith, even after not seeing him for so long: a couple of weeks ago she had heard her name on the street and saw his van moving slowly beside her as she walked, one of the front windows wound down, and then the door opened and she got in. There was no one else, he said. He'd gone back to his old room above the Indian takeaway, and it still was as it had been. He didn't want there to be anyone else; twice he repeated that. They talked for ages, he called her a star. But then he had to go.

Undressing, she caught glimpses of herself in the mirror over the unused fireplace. Her wide blue eyes glanced back at her out of features that had lost nothing of the innocence which had always been reflected in them. Hollows beneath the eyes were what she dreaded, dark as graves they could be; thankfully, she didn't have them. She turned her body so that it was in profile, one side and then the other. She was all right, she said to herself, she knew she was. All right to look at if nothing else.

In bed she lay awake, content to be there, her child quiet. A wind had got up and rattled the windows. She could hear rain too, and hearing it made being in bed a greater pleasure. She began to fall asleep but didn't quite. Everyone would be a winner, Keith used to say, even Mr Ravenswood, lonely in his old age. You had to look at it like that, he said. You had to realize, too, that all of it was for her sake more than for his own. And, most of all, for their child's sake. That day in the van he had said he understood why she hesitated, why it wasn't easy for her. He had said it gently, the way he could. He'd asked about their child.

*　*　*

Rosanne allowed a week, and then another, and part of a third to go by: thirteen working days that weren't much different from the working days that had preceded them, thirteen times to feel uneasy when she left her child with an unsatisfactory minder, and as often to resist her mother's pleas to keep out of Keith's way now that she was rid of him, to come back to Rickmansworth, which would always be her home and where everything would be easier for her.

Courage came and went on every one of the days that passed, and arguing with herself recurred on each, and in the end Rosanne went to Radcliffe Square. It was a pleasant walk one sunny lunchtime, with a sandwich in her handbag. Think of nothing, she kept telling herself. Go there, just do it, say it. Usually in her lunchtime she walked about the shops.

The square wasn't hard to find. She knew approximately where it was, and asked and was given directions. Number 81 had a white front door, a fanlight above it, white also, white pillars on either side of the steps. The name was there, beside the bell at the top, above other

names and a South American legation, and Ernst Kru-
ger Designs. A dentist and R. C. Holdings were in the
basement.

The square's railings enclosed two plane trees, several clusters of shrubs, a sunlit lawn. Rosanne crossed
the street to the gate and went in when she saw that
no one was there. The box of a lawnmower was almost
full of grass clippings, a baseball cap draped over the
mower's gear lever. There was a scattering of canvas-
seated chairs. She sat down on one of them and
unwrapped her Sandwich King sandwich.

It was impossible, though, now that she was there,
to think of nothing. Mr Ravenswood had been in the
restaurant when she'd arrived, as she had guessed he
would be, since she was late. A starchy waiter led her
to his table, although she could have managed on her
own. It was quiet, it being that kind of place. 'I used to
come here a lot once,' Mr Ravenswood had said, and
added that he hoped it wasn't an embarrassment, his
inviting her to have dinner with him. He was as polite
as he was in the bank, his manner never less than
considerate.

In the sunshine, eating her sandwich, Rosanne saw
with sudden vividness the Plume d'Or's well-separated
tables and elegant chairs, its confident waiters, heard
Mr Ravenswood asking her about herself, how she
had come to work in a bank, if she had always wanted
to do that. So long had passed, yet being close to the

house he had taken her to later that same evening nudged all this back, which startled her, for she had not expected it. 'You like our wine?' he had asked in the restaurant, putting her at her ease, and recommending white chocolate and cardamom mousse for dessert. She told him about growing up in Rickmansworth, her mother on her own, struggling to make ends meet. He spoke of his own widowhood after a happy marriage, and two children who no longer lived in England but came back often to see how he was getting on. Rosanne didn't say that for years she had been in a relationship that regularly fell apart.

From where she sat, through overhanging branches, she could see the white front door. No one came out of the house. No one entered it or rang one of the bells. She found a bin among the shrubs for the plastic that had wrapped her sandwich.

It hadn't seemed surprising when Mr Ravenswood took her arm on the street. Being in a taxi with him hadn't either, nor being in a room with quietly colourful pictures on all four walls, nor when they sat down and he poured more wine. He told her the name of the painter of the pictures. He said he collected *objets d'art* and pointed at some small bronzes on the mantelpiece. He said he hoped it hadn't been an imposition, this evening, he hadn't meant it to be that. He put on music: Brahms, he said. He asked her her other name, since only 'Rosanne' was on her plastic lapel-disc at the bank.

A man started the lawnmower and then caught sight of her. He was about to come to where she sat, began to, but changed his mind. She looked away, as if at something that had caught her eye. She told herself she shouldn't have come, that she shouldn't even be sitting where she was, in a private place. In spite of all her preparations, of waiting while determination hardened, she couldn't do what she had come to do.

She watched the grass being cut, the cumbersome machine turned in a wide curve each time another width was completed. 'Just do it,' she said aloud, the words lost in the noise, and when the lawnmower turned again she left by the open gate she had come in by.

She waited on the pavement for cars to pass. A taxi dropped children off several houses away from the one with the white front door. In the dark she hadn't noticed that it was white, or even that she had been in a square.

She pressed the bell, trying not to hope there wouldn't be an answer, then wanting there to be one when it seemed there wouldn't be.

* * *

'Yes?'

Mr Ravenswood paused before Rosanne saw him know who she was. He was dressed as she remembered, in similar clothes, including the paisley handkerchief and tie. The room he brought her to was as it had been when he'd taken her to it before, the pictures on its walls, the bronzes on the mantelpiece, the long blue curtains. The piano was open, as if someone had been playing it, music propped up.

Mr Ravenswood himself wasn't different either. The smile that had come when he'd recognized her hadn't flickered away. It didn't now.

'How have you been?' he enquired, and gestured towards the sofa where she had sat before, where she sipped more wine and told herself she shouldn't. 'Say you were passing,' Keith softly prompted. 'You saw the house, looked in to say hello.'

Rosanne said nothing. Seeking courage where she had found it already, she forced into her thoughts how it would be: Keith making it in the big-time, doing what he had a talent for, her mother saying how different he was now that he didn't have to drive a van about, now that they were settled at last. And being a mother herself, giving herself up to it, Nancy Pollitt relegated to a drab past.

Mr Ravenswood stood by the window, the light behind him, the blue of the curtains harsh where the sunshine fell on them. He didn't ask her why she had come. But still, in the way he looked and the way he spoke, he put her at her ease, as he used to in the bank.

'I didn't look after you when you were here before,' he said. 'I'm sorry.'

She watched while in silence he slightly turned

away and looked down into the square. And then the telephone rang, a faint sound, not in the room. It stopped, and then began again. Mr Ravenswood went to answer it.

* * *

Alone in the room, Rosanne said to herself she would be late. The girls would be back at their screens already, would glance up when she returned, assuming she had been delayed in some ordinary way. They didn't know about Keith. They didn't know that one of the bank's customers had once liked the look of her. She had missed out, was what they thought. She knew they did, although they didn't let it show.

Dimly and not for long, she heard Mr Ravenswood's voice. But when it ceased he did not return at once and she remembered how, that night, the lights in this room had still been on when she woke up. Her hair had kept falling over her face, her clothes had been crumpled. She'd been asleep for hours, she'd thought, but when she'd looked at her watch she'd seen that she hadn't. 'Anything could have happened,' Keith's repetition echoed. 'No way it couldn't.'

She waited, looking at the pictures she hadn't much bothered with when from politeness she had admired them. Two figures crossed a darkened road, caught by distant headlights. A woman ate alone at a kitchen table, an open book propped up against a jam jar of flowers. A man in an empty street lit a cigarette, examining suits in a shop window. The colours were muted, faded reds and faded blues, green almost grey, yellow nearly white. In Rosanne's confused recollection of being here before, she and Mr Ravenswood might have been a picture too: her wine spilt, slopping from her glass, he talking all over again about his marriage and being widowed. 'The Third,' he said, referring to the music. 'She loved it.' Rosanne had wished he hadn't put it on, had known as soon as it began that it wasn't her kind of thing.

He had been angry: suddenly he'd said that. He had been driving too fast because he had been angry. There was a quarrel, nothing much, and Rosanne had realized he was talking about his wife's death.

A Sunday afternoon, he'd said, summer. They were alone where it had happened, then people came, and cars drew up. The people – strangers – told him there'd been a death, although by now he knew there had been. He couldn't speak, could only ask, and of himself, why it could not have been he? Since he had brought it all about, why could it not have been he who had to die?

Rosanne, listening, for a moment hadn't known where she was. The music was soporific, the room was moving. The face of a man who often came to the bank was sliding about and overlapping itself; and she felt sick. 'Guilt tells you about yourself,' a voice was saying, and saying it again because she didn't understand. 'More than you want to know,' was repeated too. 'You've had a sleep,' a man who often came to the bank said.

Her coat was on the floor, as if she had been cold, as if it had been brought from where she had left it and had slipped off her. 'Well, there you are!' Keith's comment was when she told him about the coat.

Mrs Crasthorpe

On the short walk from the churchyard to her car Mrs Crasthorpe was aware of a profound humiliation. A lone mourner at her husband's funeral, she had sensed it first in the modest country church he had insisted upon for what he had called his obsequies. A woman cleric unknown to Mrs Crasthorpe had conducted a bleak service, had said the necessary words in an accent that appalled Mrs Crasthorpe, and then had scuttled off without so much as a glance in Mrs Crasthorpe's direction. Two men were waiting, leaning on their shovels in the nearby graveyard, and within minutes had returned the clay to where they had dug it from, making a little mound, the coffin gone for ever and with it Arthur, all of it a mockery. She was wrong, Mrs Crasthorpe knew, to blame Arthur for the arrangements he'd put in hand before he went, but she'd become used to blaming him in his lifetime and couldn't help doing so still.

She was a woman of fifty-nine who declared herself to be forty-five because forty-five was what she felt. She had married a considerably older man who had died in his seventy-second year. She had married him for his money, but in spite of the comfort and convenience this had brought, Mrs Crasthorpe believed that in marriage she had failed to blossom. Always a rosebud, was how, privately, she thought of herself; and there was, in Mrs Crasthorpe, a lot of privacy, there always had been. She knew she would tell no one, not ever, that Arthur had been buried without a decent send-off, just as she'd told no one that she was the mother of a son or that there had been, in the late years of her marriage, Tommy Kildare and Donald.

'I shall relish my widowhood,' she asserted, aloud and firmly, in her car. 'I shall make something of it.'

A light rain became heavier as she drove, the windscreen wipers slushing it away, a sound she particularly disliked. In the driving mirror, which she glanced at from time to time, her blonded hair, her grey-blue eyes, the curve of her generously full lips pleased Mrs Crasthorpe. She liked the look of herself, and always had.

She turned on the radio to suppress the windscreen-wiper noise, wondering as she did so why Arthur had chosen to be buried in such an obscure place, wondering what it was she hadn't listened to when she'd been told. Faintly, on some foreign station, popular music passed from tune to tune, each one known to Mrs Crasthorpe since they were of her time.

* * *

Etheridge let himself in quietly, not releasing the catch of the lock until he'd pulled it to and could open the door soundlessly. With luck, Janet would have slept and would be sleeping still. Sleep was everything to her now, the kindest friend, the tenderest lover. She didn't allow it to be induced, the drugs she was offered invariably declined.

He looked down at the sleeping face that illness was taking from him, a little more each day. For a moment he saw in the wan, tired features the shadows of Juliet, the wisdom of Portia, Estella's thoughtless pride. 'I'll go,' the carer whispered from the doorway.

'Dear Janet,' he whispered himself, wondering how her day had been.

When he had made tea Etheridge carried the tray back to the bedside and the rattle of the cup and saucer woke his wife, as every day it did. It was what Janet wanted, what she liked: that she should always be awake when he was here.

'Hello again,' she said.

He bent to embrace her, and held her for a moment in his arms, then plumped her pillows up and straightened the turndown of her top sheet. She said, when he asked, that she was feeling better. But she didn't eat any of the cake he had brought, or the biscuits, and didn't look as well as she had that morning.

'Oh, nothing to write home about,' he responded to a query of how the day had been for him. She'd

finished *A Fine Balance*, she said. She'd heard a pro-
gramme about silverware on the radio. 'Well, no,' she
said. 'Not interesting at all.'

'Some soup later, darling? Cream cracker?'

'Soup would be lovely. No cream cracker.'

'We landed the contract. I thought we wouldn't.'

'I knew you would.'

She was an actress. He had been settled for years in
the offices of Forrester and Bright, a firm of specialist
printers that had made a corner for itself by taking on
complicated assignments which other printers couldn't
be bothered with. In their early forties now, they'd
been married since they were both twenty-three.

'It's awful for you,' Janet said, gloomy as she sometimes was when she'd just woken up.

'Of course it isn't.' Without an effort, the familiar
reassurance came.

They smiled at one another. They knew it was
awful.

'*University Challenge* tonight,' Janet said.

*   *   *

'You'll behave yourself,' the warder said.

'I always do.'

'She's here. You see you do.'

Derek wished she wouldn't come. All of it was silly
from both their points of view. She knew it was, it
wasn't as if she didn't, but still she came. She'd tell him

the latest about the old boy and he'd try not to hear. She'd tell him because there was nothing else to tell him. She'd sit there in her finery, ashamed of him and ashamed because she was. She had called it naughty once, the way he was. She didn't call it anything now.

He heard the click of her heels, a sprightly sound, different from the thump of boots. The warder respected her, knowing her from her visits; a nice man, she said. She liked people being nice.

'Now, you behave, lad.' The warder again rebuked Derek in advance, a white splotch on the shiny peak of his cap his only untidiness.

'You see that?' Derek said when she came. 'A bird done its business on Mr Fane.'

He teased her with bad grammar and she winced when he did although she pretended she didn't mind. She was on about something new: the old boy had died and no one had come to the funeral. Derek hadn't known him, there had never been a reason why they should have known one another, but even so she talked about him.

'You all right?' she asked.

'Oh, great,' he said.

* * *

And that was all; Mrs Crasthorpe accepted without protest that their brief exchanges were over. 'You're good, the way you come,' the warder said when she began to go. She left a pot of damson jam, which was a favourite.

She hailed a taxi and asked to be taken to Pasmore's. She had phoned, as she always did, to make sure there'd be a table for her, and there it was, in the corner she had come to regard as hers. They didn't gush in Pasmore's; you could feel the dignity of their being above it. They spoke almost in whispers, but you could hear every word because they wanted you to. She always had tea in Pasmore's after visiting Derek.

Ordering from the waitress who had come at once to her, her thoughts picked up from where she'd left them, no different from the thoughts she always had in Pasmore's. He couldn't help himself, he didn't try. He wasn't the kind to try, he had explained: he liked being a persistent offender. Yet even so it couldn't be less than horrid for him. That it must be awful had many times haunted Mrs Crasthorpe at this same table, and she pressed it away from her now, glancing about for a face she recognized among the teatime people. But, as always, there wasn't one.

'How nice!' She smiled away her dejection when her sultana scones came and her tea was poured for her, which they always did for one at Pasmore's.

*　*　*

When Janet died, painlessly in her sleep, Etheridge moved from the flat in Barnes to a smaller one in

Weymouth Street, no practicality or economic neces-
sity inspiring the change. It was just that Barnes,
shadowed now by death, was not as once it had been.
Its spaciousness, its quiet streets, stared back at Etheridge morosely, the jazz pub that had been theirs
seeming ordinary, the river unappealing. The same
flowers blooming again in the window boxes should
have been a memory and a solace, but were not. Moving in at Weymouth Street, Etheridge thought of
leaving Forrester and Bright, of leaving London too,
but when a few weeks had gone by Weymouth Street
seemed far enough. It had no past, it tugged at nothing. He settled there.

* * *

Mrs Crasthorpe set about making something special
of her widowhood with a will. She spent a week in
Eastbourne clarifying her thoughts, for the town's
modest opulence, its unhurried peace and sense of
other times had had a calming effect before. Nothing
had changed: the Parades, the Grand Hotel, the well-
dressed people on the streets, the unfearful sea drew
once more from Mrs Crasthorpe an admiration that
went back to her girlhood. It was in Eastbourne she
first had felt the better for being alive. She could think
more productively in the briny air, she got things
right. Funeral weeds had had their day, solemn rites
were dead and gone: in the dining room of the Grand

Hotel she sensed she was forgiven for her unshed tears, the grief she could not manage. Shambling through his days, Arthur hadn't wanted to know about Tommy Kildare or Donald. 'We're chalk and cheese,' he said vaguely. He left her everything.

She walked about in Eastbourne, going nowhere, wondering if she would meet a chum and when she didn't it seemed better that she shouldn't, that privately and on her own she should dwell on how life should be now. In this she did not banish fantasy: her chums would give her a party, for they were party people. In twos and threes they would stand about and see in her another woman, and Derek would come with presents, as he never had before; and Tommy Kildare would be as once he'd been. So young she seemed, he'd say, she could be seventeen. And Donald would kiss her fingers and call himself a Regency buck.

*   *   *

At first Etheridge didn't hang up the print of Seurat's *Sunday Afternoon* when he moved to Weymouth Street, but then he did because it was a shame not to. Framed and wrapped, it had been waiting for him one 12 September, probably his fortieth, he thought. The sum of the accumulated IOUs, each one dated 4 April, hadn't become enough for Janet's earrings; they would have if there'd been another year. Sometimes, even in Weymouth Street, such lesser shadows flitted about, but

Etheridge dismissed this interference as a trick of the light or of his own imagination.

Work was a help, and when he had been in Weymouth Street for less than six months he ceased to lie sleepless in the lonely early hours. Recollections were less distinct; bits of remembered conversations were somehow lost, the last of the clothes were given away. At a cookery class he learnt to make risotto and eggs Benedict. He played the piano more skilfully than before, had a drink every evening in the Cock and Lion, read Mauriac in French and was promoted at Forrester and Bright.

* * *

Mrs Crasthorpe had earlier noticed somewhere the man who was coming towards her in Beaumont Street. His tie bore the colours of a regiment or public school. His hands were delicate: gentle hands, Mrs Crasthorpe surmised, the fingernails well kept. He had looks, and she imagined charm; she liked the way he dressed. She liked his serious expression as he walked, how he seemed to dwell on serious matters, unravelling confusion, clever. He wasn't in a hurry. She liked that too.

'Enford Crescent,' she said to herself, wondering how long it was since Enford Crescent had been plucked out of nowhere by Tups or Primmie, she couldn't remember which. You asked the way to Enford Crescent when a boy you liked the look of came along. He wouldn't know, he couldn't know: there was no Enford Crescent. For an hour once Primmie and a nameless boy had trailed about, searching for what they would never find, falling in love, so Primmie had said. And Tups another time, searching also, was taken to the Palm Grove, and bought a Peach Surprise.

*   *   *

'I think it's probably quite near,' Etheridge said when he was asked for directions to somewhere he thought he'd once noticed on a street sign. 'Excuse me,' he called out to a couple with a dog on a lead. 'This lady's looking for Enford Crescent.'

The couple had been engaged in an argumentative conversation which had abruptly ceased. They were middle-aged and tired-looking, a note of impatience in both their voices. The dog was a black-and-white smooth-haired fox terrier, snappish because it disliked its lead.

'Enford?' the man who restrained it repeated. 'Not round here, I shouldn't think.'

His companion nodded her agreement. The woman who'd asked for directions was smiling rather helplessly now, Etheridge thought. 'Never mind,' she said.

The couple and the dog went on. 'You've been most kind,' the woman in search of Enford Crescent said.

'Well, hardly that.'

'Oh, yes. Indeed.'

'I'm sorry I misled you.'

'No, no.'

'Someone will know when you ask again.'

'Of course.'

* * *

Mrs Crasthorpe watched the man she had spoken to walking away from her, and when he passed out of sight she missed him as if she knew him. He had a cultivated voice and was polite without being like an icicle. She'd always been attracted by fair-haired men.

Still gazing into the empty distance, she felt the weight of her middle age. She'd been impulsive once upon a time, hasty and not caring that she was. Tups had called her a spur-of-the-moment girl. Primmie had too. They'd liked impulsiveness in her; she'd liked it herself. He would have done, the fair-haired man, she'd known he would. She would have told him. He would have listened and understood. She knew that too and yet she'd let him go.

* * *

For no particular reason, when Janet was ill, Etheridge had begun to fill the remaining pages of a half-used-up ledger book with autobiographical jottings. He did not intend this to be a diary, simply a record of early childhood, his own and Janet's, some later memories collected too. It established time and place, what had been shared and what had not, the marriage, and people known and houses lived in. While he was homesick at a Gloucestershire boarding school, Janet was being taught at home by a Miss Francis, school for a delicate child being considered a risk. Her first theatrical appearance, unnamed, unnoticed, was in the pantomime chorus of *Jack and the Beanstalk*. Short-skirted, glamorous, she was seventeen, while Etheridge, not then known to her, was waiting for a vocation to offer itself. They met when Janet came to London.

Alone thirty years later, Etheridge could not forgive her death and imagined he never would. He sensed that his feelings were unreasonable and he struggled to dismiss them, disliking himself for what seemed to be a selfishness. But still resentment hung about. Why should she not have what mostly people did have, why was she now mere dust?

The autumn that came was an Indian summer and every weekend, on either Saturday or Sunday, Etheridge walked in Regent's Park. He learnt from a book the names of flowers he didn't know, he fed the birds. But mainly, while time passed more slowly than on weekdays, he watched from a pavement table of a café the people who came and went. He envied them, and he envied himself as he had been.

* * *

When years ago, and halfway through her marriage, Mrs Crasthorpe discovered this same part of London she liked it at once. She had visited it to inspect, and take her pick of, an elderly woman's jewellery, the woman once well-to-do but no longer. Mrs Crasthorpe had bought three rings and a bracelet and when, a month or so later, the same advertisement appeared again she made a second journey and persuaded her husband on her return to sell their house and buy one she had seen in Coppice Mews. She liked the mews, she liked the streets and so did he; he hadn't at first but with time she persuaded him that he did. He died in Coppice Mews, apologizing for having to leave her on her own and for wanting to be buried in a small country churchyard she considered unsuitable for the urban man he'd been. She honoured his wishes none the less, and was already on familiar terms with the people of the shops, had the mews house painted in the colours she had previously wanted. All of which, for Mrs Crasthorpe, increased the pleasure of widowhood.

* * *

A faintly familiar face was what Etheridge was aware of, without knowing where or when he'd seen it before. Then he remembered and nodded at the woman who was turning the pages of a newspaper at the next table. She stared at him when he did so, as if her thoughts had been similar to his. 'Good Lord!' a moment later she exclaimed. Her scent was as pungent as it had been when she had asked for directions. Her clothes were different. She held out a hand that was just within Etheridge's reach. 'I rather think we've met before,' she said.

'Well, yes, we have.'

'What weather!'

'It's lovely.'

'A day for the races!'

She used to go racing often, she said. The Oaks, the Derby, Cheltenham. Wimbledon for the tennis, Henley. 'Oh, such a lot,' she said, but things were quieter now. Inevitable, of course, as the years pile up.

She was handsome in her fleshy way, Etheridge supposed. Careful, experienced. You couldn't call her gross, and there was something in her lavish, well-used smile that was almost delicate. Her teeth were very white. Her breasts were firm, her knees were trim. She fiddled with a brooch she wore, a loop of tiny stones, chips of sapphire and washed-out ruby they might have been, the only decoration on a pale cream dress. Sometimes a languid look came into her features and for a moment then they were tranquil.

'What a troublesome country Cambodia is!' she chattily remarked, folding away her newspaper as she spoke. 'You'd think they'd have more sense.'

She was the worst in the world about names, she confided, seeming to imply that Etheridge had told her his on their previous encounter, which he hadn't. His coffee came, too hot to be drunk in a couple of gulps, allowing him to go away.

* * *

It was extraordinary, Mrs Crasthorpe marvelled, that he should again be here, this attractive stranger who had continued to float about in her consciousness, and whom she'd made herself love a little. What lengths she went to, she reflected, how determinedly she guarded herself from the cruelty that was more than Tommy Kildare's treachery or Donald deciding he was homosexual, more than the haunting years of Arthur's dreary world, more than tediousness and boredom. How good the everyday was, the ordinary with its lesser tribulations and simple pleasures. 'What are you thinking?' she asked.

Unable to find the white lies that were always there for him, Etheridge muttered incomprehensibly. He wondered if this talkative woman was drunk, but the flow of information about herself had come in an orderly manner, suggesting that she was not.

'How attractive your name is,' she said. 'Crasthorpe is appalling, don't you think?'

She had been Georgina Gilmour once, she said, the same Gilmours who had carried their name all over the English-speaking world. The Crasthorpes had never been much and were, of course, unrelated to her.

'How much I enjoy conversation with strangers,' in passing she revealed.

She spoke about the Gilmours at some length, their place in Scotland for the shooting, the child among them in the past who'd been a musical genius, and Nanny Fortescue to whom three generations had been devoted, and old Wyse Gilmour who'd raced at Silverstone and lived to be a hundred and two.

'Well, there you are,' she said, without finality. She scribbled on the edge of her newspaper and handed him the scrap of paper she tore off: she'd written down her address.

'We clearly are not birds of a feather,' pensively she concluded. 'But if you should ever think we might know one another better I'm nearly always at home in the afternoon.'

He nodded vaguely. Abrupt and dogmatic, her manner might have seemed rude, but she managed to make it an unawareness, as probably it was.

'Your wife,' she said. 'You mentioned your wife.'

He shook his head.

'I thought you said your wife . . .'

'No.'

'I thought . . .'

'My wife died.'

*   *   *

84

Afterwards, Etheridge avoided having coffee at that particular café, but several times he caught a glimpse of Mrs Crasthorpe, once coming out of the Cock and Lion. It had surprised him when she'd said they weren't birds of a feather: he had imagined that was what she'd thought they were. He avoided the Cock and Lion too, and frequented instead the Admiral's Rest, which was further away and rougher. Once he heard his name called out in Vincent Street and walked more quickly on. Mrs Crasthorpe did not interest or concern him, and it was hard to believe that this pushy, over-lively woman might possess qualities more appealing than her manner. Crowded out by his continuing anger at the careless greed of death, her attentions were hardly noticed. Mrs Crasthorpe would fade away to nothing, as she had been before she asked him for directions.

But having lunch at Le Paon one day with the two men from the office he regularly had lunch with, he thought he saw Mrs Crasthorpe on the street. The plate-glass terrace doors of the restaurant had not been folded back, as in high summer they invariably were: Le Paon in early autumn echoed only with its own mur-mur of voices, enlivened with occasional laughter. All three men had ordered chops; a glass of house wine had been brought to each. Their conversation while they waited was devoted to the difficulties that had arisen because a typeface was neither available nor obtainable. 'I'll try Thompson's this afternoon,' one of Etheridge's colleagues said, and the other mentioned J. Sinclair's in Edinburgh. Etheridge said nothing.

Mrs Crasthorpe wasn't wearing her pale cream dress, but instead a flowery one he had also become familiar with. She was standing still, in conversation with a figure in a long black overcoat which looked, at least from a distance, to be much too heavy for the time of year. Its wearer – his back to the restaurant's façade and to Etheridge – gestured repeatedly, as if in persuasion. Mrs Crasthorpe did not seem happy. From time to time she attempted to move away, only to be drawn back by her companion's insistence that their encounter should continue.

'Your chops, sir,' a waiter said, and there were roast potatoes and parsnips mashed and rich brown gravy.

'Or possibly Langford's.' Etheridge at last contributed something to what was being discussed, feeling that he should.

When the meal ended he noticed that while he hadn't been looking the conversation on the street appeared to have become a fracas. Mrs Crasthorpe and the man in the black coat were now the centre of a small crowd, the man still gesturing, Mrs Crasthorpe more agitated than before. Etheridge could hear the voices of several bystanders raised in angry abuse that was clearly directed at the blackly clad figure. Two elderly women pushed to get closer to him; a bearded man was restrained from striking him; a younger woman was shouting into a mobile telephone. Then the gesticulating ceased and the man in the black coat shrugged, his arms raised in despair, his comic stance suggesting that something he considered to be a source of humour had been misunderstood. Etheridge didn't feel the incident was worth drawing to his colleagues' attention and by the time he reached the street himself the crowd had disappeared and Mrs Crasthorpe had too. The man in the black coat was laughing, his wrists held out to the two policemen who had taken charge of him.

* * *

Unnatural little bastard, the warder's unspoken thought was when he heard this arrest had taken place. His own mother, the thought went on, who brought him jam and did her best. His own mother, and in broad daylight.

* * *

'Only teasing,' Derek said the next time she came. 'I thought you'd be amused.'

* * *

She wept where no one could see her. She never had where anyone could, not ever in all the days and nights, all the waking up to another incident and Arthur knowing nothing. She hadn't wept when Tommy Kildare had had enough of her or when Donald needed something different. But she wept her private tears whenever she imagined the coat unbuttoned, the sudden twitch as it opened wide, the torch's flash. She wept because she loved him as she did no other human being. She always had. She always would.

* * *

In time Etheridge married again, a relationship that strengthened as more time passed, his contentment in it similar to the contentment he had discovered in marriage before. It seemed natural in the circumstances to move away from Weymouth Street and he did so; natural, too, to buy a house in quiet Petersham, rescuing it from years of neglect and subsequent decay. A child was born there, and then another.

To his second wife Etheridge talked about his first, which caused neither offence nor irritation, and even the bitter chagrin of his mourning was understood. He considered himself fortunate in almost every aspect of his life as it now was, in his wife and his children, in the position he held at Forrester and Bright, in the open sward of Petersham, its city buses plying daily, its city sounds a whisper in a quieter London.

Another winter passed, another spring, and most of summer. August became September and it was then, as the days were shortening, that the name Crasthorpe occurred again. The name was unusual and it caught Etheridge's eye in a newspaper item concerning a woman who in the night had fallen down in the street and had lain there until she was discovered by refuse collectors when the dusk of another early morning came. She had died while being conveyed to hospital in the refuse men's enormous vehicle, a reek of whisky emanating from her sodden clothes. Cold print reported a scene that moved him: a shrunken body gently placed on its bed of waste, the refuse men standing awkwardly then, saying nothing. The woman was thought to be a vagrant, but Etheridge saw blonded hair bedraggled and stockinged knees, an easy smile and clothes he remembered. Chatter he'd been unable to escape from he remembered too: childhood friends recalled, and going to the races, and conversations with strangers. He'd thrown away the scrap of paper that had been pressed upon him, its sprawl of handwriting unread. In Vincent Street he had hurried on.

But the curiosity Mrs Crasthorpe had failed to inspire in her lifetime came now. Why had she lain all night where she had fallen? Why were her clothes saturated with whisky, she who had been so conventional and respectable? What did her wordless epitaph say?

* * *

Lost somewhere in the crowded tangle bound by Mare Street, Morning Lane and Urswick Road is unmarked Falter Way, the sign that once identified it claimed by vandals long ago. It is a narrow passage, not greatly used because it terminates abruptly and leads nowhere. No street lights burn at night in Falter Way, no brass plate or printed notice proclaims the practice of commerce or a profession. There are no shops in Falter Way, no bars, no breakfast cafés. No enterprising business girls hang about in doorways.

'Crasthorpe.' A uniformed policeman repeated the name and shrugged away his dismay.

'Poor bloody woman,' his colleague said, and closed his notebook.

There was nothing untoward to report, nothing to add or alter. What had happened here was evident and apparent, without a trace of anything that needed to be looked at more carefully.

In turn the two men telephoned, then went away.

*   *   *

Derek wondered why his mother didn't come and hoped it was because at last she'd realized that all of it was ridiculous. When the old boy died she'd said, 'Come to the house,' and he hadn't understood that she meant to live there. She could pass him off as a houseboy, her idea was; she couldn't see the snags.

Once she would have said snags didn't matter. Once she'd liked being teased. Funny, how she was.

*   *   *

Etheridge found it hard to forget Mrs Crasthorpe, although he wanted to. It shamed him that he had thought so little of her, a woman not really known to him, and then only because she'd been embarrassing and even a nuisance. He had read about Falter Way in the newspaper report of her death and had wondered why she had gone there. On an impulse, when months afterwards he was near it himself, he asked about Mrs Crasthorpe and although she was remembered no one had known her name. In nearby Dring Street and the shoddy bars of Breck Hill he imagined her, a different woman, drinking heavily. She went with men, a barman said, she liked a man.

Etheridge guessed his way through the mystery of Mrs Crasthorpe, but too much was missing and he resisted further speculation. He sensed his own pity, not knowing why it was there. He honoured a tiresome woman's secret and saw it kept.

The Unknown Girl

For hardly longer than a second the people on the pavement's edge were frozen in perfect stillness. Then a man stepped into the oncoming traffic, both arms peremptorily raised to halt it. The driver's door of the green-and-yellow van that had so dramatically braked while lurching to one side now opened. A voice called for an ambulance. 'St Wistan Street,' someone else added, and the halted traffic was beckoned on.

'There is no pulse,' a woman kneeling beside the figure on the ground said, but even so a rolled-up overcoat was placed beneath the lolling head.

In the double-decker bus that had been stopped and again was moving, strangers spoke to one another, staring out at the scene that had so quickly come about. The driver of the van was distressed and expostulating; the uninvolved had gathered on the tarmacked surface, exchanging their versions of how the occurrence might have come about. Some, who'd seen nothing, asked what had happened and were differently answered. An ambulance came, so quickly it was commented on. A stretcher was laid down, ready for its burden. A man pushed in, causing people incorrectly to remark that he would be a doctor. A police car, dawdling until now, drew in behind the ambulance. The body was covered with a blanket on the stretcher, the ambulance doors were softly closed. This life was over.

* * *

Some days after the tragedy in St Wistan Street Harriet Balfour opened her front door to a stooped, frail man in clerical dress whom she did not know. He asked if she was Mrs Balfour and, when she said she was, asked if he might speak to her. Harriet took him to her drawing room. She was in a hurry, for the mornings were her busy time, but she did not say so. In the drawing room she offered coffee instead.

A quiet beauty distinguished the middle age of Harriet Balfour, gaining something in maturity, as much as it had lost of girlhood's prettiness. Obedient to her vanity, the grey in her hair was softened in an artificial way, her skin was daily cared for, its small ravages patiently repaired. Colours were worn because they suited her; a modest manner, and hesitation before putting forth a view, governed youth's impetuosity now, becoming a tranquillity that was attractive in itself.

A son, education over, her only child, still lived with her; but, widowed now, Harriet knew that one day she would be alone in a house she had grown increasingly to love, which she had come to when she was rescued from a relationship that had failed, a

house where she had borne her child into a contentment that continued until, too soon, her husband had
died. Her attachment to the house had much to do
with her devotion to his memory, and she predicted
that she would not wish to move away, nor allow whatever ailments time brought to dictate otherwise. No
matter what, the past she had known here would never
be less than it had been – in the rooms of the house,
and in the airy garden where Comice pears loosened
every autumn, and lacy hydrangeas decorated faded
brick, and blowsy Victorian roses thrived. There would
always be the John Piper in the hall, the Minton in the
drawing room, and waking to the wisteria of a faded
wallpaper she had particularly come to know.

She might have married again, but the suggestion,
when more than once it was put to her, seemed absurd:
apart from love remembered, there was already
enough in Harriet's life. She listened to music, took
pains with cooking, gardened, kept up with friends.
In Italy the early and mid-Renaissance delighted her.
In France the Impressionists did. She read the novels
that time's esteem had kept alive, and judged contemporary fiction for herself.

'No, no, not coffee, thank you,' the clergyman
declined her hospitality. He apologized for disturbing
her, then explained why he had come. 'Your name
and address were on a cleaner's work-list.' He gave the
cleaner's name.

'Yes, Emily Vance came here,' Harriet agreed when she heard it. 'She doesn't any more. She hasn't for quite a while, nine or ten months.'

'Emily Vance died, Mrs Balfour. Tragically, in a street accident.'

Harriet, who had not sat down, did so now. 'My God, how terrible!' she said, and at once felt embarrassed because she had expressed herself in language unsuitable for a clergyman to have to hear. But he was unperturbed.

'I do not seek to involve you, Mrs Balfour,' he said. 'It's simply that nothing appears to be known about the girl. Little more than her name.'

He had realized when he heard about the accident that this might be a person who had sometimes come to his church. Though never to a service, he said, which made it seem as if the reason for her coming was simply to be alone. He'd been told by the police when he made enquiries that she had lived in the flat of a foreign couple, above a stationer's shop in Camona Street. A note of the address was found on a library card in the handbag that was afterwards picked up where it had fallen.

'Camona Street's not in my parish,' he said, 'but even so it was my church she came to – perhaps because it is out of the way and ill-attended. I went to see the foreign couple, I felt I had to. In the four years Emily Vance had been their lodger, they told me she'd had no visitors, had not once used the telephone, received no letters and, listening, I realized that this was indeed the girl who had found some kind of sanctuary in the corner of a shadowy pew in a church.'

The clergyman introduced himself then, apologizing for not doing so before, giving a name that sounded like Malfrey. He was older than Harriet had first thought, and she felt sorry for him, a thankless task imposed upon him because there was no one else.

'Sanctuary?' She repeated his word, since she hadn't understood its implications at the time.

'Well, yes, I think so. The couple in Camona Street asked me if I would conduct her funeral. But of course there would be a family somewhere and I've been trying to find out what might be known from the people she cleaned for.'

'Of course. I understand. But all I can tell you is that Emily wasn't the kind to talk about herself, which you may have guessed already. She did the work well, better than most. But it did occasionally cross my mind that it was strange she should be a cleaner. I used to think she had fallen on hard times.'

'Yes, there was apparently that feeling.'

'She left us and that was that. One morning she simply didn't come.'

'I'm sorry to bring all this to you, Mrs Balfour.'

The slow, clerical enunciation went on a bit. The address of a church – the Church of St John the

Evangelist – was given, and then the day and the time of the funeral.

'But how did it happen? An accident?' Harriet asked when they both stood up.

She led the clergyman back through the hall while he repeated at second-hand what had been described to him. The driver of a van – delivering flowers, it was thought – had denied negligence. The proprietor of a betting shop had been about to cross the street also, but the pedestrian light had changed to red. The girl had gone on, he said, not waiting, as he and everyone else had. The van had been in a traffic filter and had come unexpectedly and perhaps too fast. But in spite of someone saying afterwards that there was drink on the driver's breath it was generally felt that he could not be blamed. It had almost seemed deliberate, the betting-shop proprietor had said, the way the girl hadn't waited for the light to change.

'I'm sorry,' the clergyman apologized. 'I have distressed you, Mrs Balfour.'

'It doesn't matter. Thank you for coming.'

* * *

Harriet wished he hadn't. All that morning, doing her weekly stint at the Oxfam shop, she wished he hadn't. Sorting books that had recently been left, she put aside *Around the World in Eighty Days* to read sometime to the old men of the Soldiers' and Sailors' Home. She listened to Miss Chantry bringing her up to date on her brother-in-law's angina. She arranged for shoes and garments, no use to anyone, to be disposed of. But increasingly she felt haunted by the spare, elderly features of the clergyman who had briefly been an awkward presence in her drawing room. He had said that Emily Vance had always paid the rent promptly where she lived, that she came and went so quietly she was hardly noticed, that she was no trouble.

After she left the Oxfam shop, and with time on her hands, Harriet had coffee in Caffè Nero before she began the long walk back to her house. Emily Vance had been a special person: often she had thought so. Dark-haired and sombre, as quiet as the clergyman described, she'd been attractive in an unaffected way, her delicate features arranged in an oval that made the most of them. Conscientious as an employee, she'd been a godsend too. Yet, without a word beforehand or a note sent afterwards, she had one day not come back.

Timing her lunchtime boiled egg, brown-bread slices toasting, Harriet remembered searching, bewildered, for an explanation and deciding that none she found was entirely likely. She had banished conjecture then, since it was no more than that and offered nothing. But today, while listening to Miss Chantry passing on the newest details of her brother-in-law's angina, and in the Caffè Nero, and now, the same conjecture nagged, its source the contents of a moment.

She'd been on the way downstairs. In the hall Emily Vance was washing the tiles, Stephen, passing, tiptoeing across the wet floor. No glance that Harriet had seen had been exchanged by the two, no words, no gesture. But Emily Vance who did not often smile had smiled when again she was on her own, as if recalling a moment of pleasure. There was no more than that, but still Harriet had wondered, and wondered now more than she had before. Only weeks had passed before her cleaner had failed to come back.

She told herself, as she had then, that she was being fanciful. Deception was not Stephen's way and surely it was straining speculation to assume that, as well as a clandestine relationship, there had been a quarrel that brought it to an end; that her son, unlike herself, had been careless in what he'd said. Anxiety played cruel tricks, she sensibly reminded herself.

It was still early – not yet three – when she began to read another chapter of *Beau Geste* to the old men of the Soldiers' and Sailors' Home. Afterwards she stayed with them for a little longer because they liked to talk about what they had heard, or simply liked to talk, and reminisce.

It was then, while listening to their memories, that the nagging began again. It would go, she thought, but it didn't, and it didn't while she waved goodbye to the little group that had formed.

The afternoon was fine, pale April sunlight

glancing off shop-window glass and the façades of houses, dipping into trim front gardens. But before Harriet reached the Common – which was the pleasantest part of the walk – she changed her mind about going home immediately and waited for a bus that went in the opposite direction.

It took her ages to find Camona Street but when she did she saw the stationer's shop at once and was told the stairs to the flat above it were through a storage room at the back. She hesitated then, among stacks of packaged paper and cardboard boxes in piles, and jars of glue, and chalk and ballpoint pens, tied-up waste bags. People talking, she said to herself, no more than that it would have been, people saying anything, adding something extra to the drama that had so suddenly happened. The clergyman had been cautious, not stating in any certain way that Emily Vance had taken her life.

'Up there is what you want.' Appearing suddenly, the man who'd directed her to the back of the shop pointed at uncarpeted stairs. The smell of food recently cooked drifted down to them. Harriet nodded and went up as she was directed.

* * *

They did not sit down. The man, who was thin and small with pallid features, kept turning away, a wiry jerkiness about his movements. The woman was small too, with bushy grey hair falling to her shoulders.

'She had the rooms,' the woman said. 'Two rooms, the door between, the bathroom she could use.'

Harriet was shown the table on which Emily Vance's handbag had been examined by people who came after the accident. Police it was who emptied the handbag there.

'No need they should do that,' the woman said.

The man added that Emily Vance had said she was a cleaner of people's houses when first she came to ask about the rooms. A silence completed these revelations, and then Harriet said, 'There has apparently been talk about whether or not your lodger took her life. Do you think perhaps she did?'

That brought no comment, except, again, that they did not know, that they were not there, that they had witnessed nothing. One and then the other said it. But as Harriet was leaving, the door held open for her, she was told that in all the time Emily Vance had lived in the two rooms she had not ever sat with them in the evening, not even once. They spoke about this inadequacy together too, one speaking, then the other, their disappointment shared.

'Such a thing on the street,' the woman said.

* * *

In her kitchen Harriet lifted down plates to be warmed in the oven later, and her heavy blue casserole dish. She assembled what otherwise she needed for her cooking, and opened wine. She chopped up parsley, washed celery stalks and mushrooms, measured out a cup of rice. Smoke curled for a moment from the oil she heated, she seared the meat she had sliced. She poured out cream and turned on the machine that whipped it for her. Her own confection of apricots and Cointreau had earlier been prepared.

It surely could not have been much, she thought, whatever there had been, if there'd been anything. Nor was there any reason why she should imagine otherwise just because of today. The clergyman expected her to attend the funeral, and she would. For his sake, because he had come quite a long way, because he was doing his best. But even so Harriet wished she hadn't brought him to the drawing room and allowed him to get going. She should have kept him at the door, the way you had to with Jehovah's Witnesses. She wished she had done that.

Dvořák was on the radio when she turned it on and with time on her hands, for she had got on well, she sat down and listened to it. The last movement ended just before her son called out from the hall, saying he was back.

*　*　*

'What kind of a day?' Fair-haired and lanky, Stephen carried their two heated plates, with the casserole, to the dining room. Harriet followed with rice and broccoli.

'Oh, nothing much,' she said. There'd been the shopping, her visit to the old men, and walking back across the Common in the evening. She didn't mention anything else.

'How good you are to people!' Softly spoken, Stephen sounded like his father, who had often said Harriet was good. They both remembered that and Stephen smiled, as if they had said more. Harriet shook her head, which had been her response to the compliment in the past.

'I like this chicken,' Stephen commented, pouring more wine for both of them.

Several times in the course of the day Harriet had wondered about mentioning the clergyman's visit. Before she finished in the Oxfam shop she had begun to think she wouldn't, and had thought so again later, and later still, after she had been to Camona Street. She knew it would be more interesting to recount her day more fully, as usually she did, to pass on the bad news it had brought. 'There's money in a drawer,' the woman in Camona Street had said. 'Would do for a funeral.'

But at dinner they talked of other matters, easily, lightly, for conversation was never difficult, and this evening, as on other evenings, an undemanding affection one for the other made their relationship more than it might have been. Their closeness came naturally, neither through obligation nor for a reason that was not one of feeling; and it was never said, but only known, that different circumstances, coming naturally also, would change everything. They lived in a time-being, and accepted that.

In the kitchen they shared the washing-up, and Stephen laid the table there, ready for breakfast. He had achondroplasia to read up on, he said, and tonight he would rather do that than watch television or whatever. His father had been a paediatrician. He was to be one himself.

* * *

Sir Felix had his work to do, and was willing to do it – as far as such willingness could go with him . . . Harriet slept then, taking Sir Felix and his work with her, the page open on her pillow. A moment later, her book fell and woke her. Leaving it where it was, she turned the light off.

And Stephen, finishing with achondroplasia an hour later, stretched and yawned, undressed and washed and went to bed. He slept at once.

There was no movement then in the house that once Emily Vance had cleaned. No mice crept about, for what mice there were had eaten unwisely all that had been left out for them and were no longer alive.

No would-be burglar tried the windows. No cats came to the garden, careless of the broken glass that crowned its high walls. Nor was the spectre of Emily Vance anywhere, neither in the house nor in the garden, where she'd so often been urged to sit in the sun for her coffee, to pick the lily of the valley when it was profuse, and daffodils before they drooped. Emily Vance was not in dreams and came back only with the light of dawn, alive in Harriet's memory as yesterday returned. But what had yesterday attracted unease and doubt was calmly presented now, and Harriet was calm herself. She did not fret. With a precision free of apprehension, she saw again her cleaner kneeling in the hall, her sodden cloth completing her washing of the red-and-black tiles. The front door banged as Stephen left the house and this morning it seemed to Harriet that what she had witnessed – more likely than a secret concealed – was the shyness of undeclared love. And she imagined her cleaner delighting in the pinned-up photographs on the walls of Stephen's bedroom, and in his bedside books, and the reproduction he had framed himself of Bonnard's boats, the postcard portrait of Anna Akhmatova, his pop-singer fish that sang a song. His shirts and ties were stroked, his pillow smoothed, his overcoat settled on its hanger. How often had the heady thrill of his voice, his laughter, come from somewhere else in the house and been the moment of the day? How often was the cup he'd drunk from washed up last, so precious was the unseen imprint of his lips?

These snatches of illusion crowded Harriet's consciousness and, though touched by death because death had come, they offered a consolation that continued. She was right to say nothing, for why should Stephen bear a burden that was not his to bear? She slept again, more deeply than before, and woke at seven.

The air was cold in the garden when she walked there, the early-morning noise of the city muffled. She tidied a flowerbed, picked the last of the double-headed narcissi and brought them to the kitchen. There would be a funeral. The episode would end with that.

* * *

An organist played Bach and then was silent. The clergyman who had broken the news of the death to Harriet spoke old-fashioned words that still were beautiful and she knew that that was why they had been chosen.

She had come to the funeral not only because she felt it was expected of her but because she expected it of herself. In the church there were two other women, each on her own, found no doubt as she'd been found. The couple from Camona Street were there.

'"For a thousand years in thy sight are but as yesterday ... as soon as thou scatterest them, they are even as a sleep: and fade away suddenly like the grass."'

Beautiful as the words were, they seemed not to belong. A week had passed since the clergyman's visit but time, accumulating, had contributed nothing. Neither to the life there had been nor to the death, and in this place, which isolated the spiritual and honoured it, no truth began.

'"In the morning it is green, and groweth up: but in the evening it is cut down, dried up, and withered . . . all our days are gone: we bring our years to an end, as it were a tale that is told."'

The voice echoed, the name at last was spoken. In a whisper at the door as Harriet entered the church, she had been asked if she was aware of another given name; but she knew only Emily, and so that alone was used.

'"In the midst of life we are in death. Thou knowest, Lord, the secrets of our hearts . . ."'

No hymn was sung. There was no eulogy, and the coffin remained when the service ended later, to be conveyed to the crematorium.

'Thank you for coming.' In the awkward pause there was outside the church the old clergyman said the same to everyone. 'You'll take a little tea with me?' half-heartedly he invited.

The two women who were also on their own apologized for their presence, each murmuring her appreciation of the service. The couple from Camona Street went away quickly. A limping sexton carried out the flowers.

'It was too little,' the clergyman said. His name was on a board in front of the church, gold letters on black. *The Reverend C. R. Malfrey.* 'Too slight. Too empty.'

'No. No, not at all,' Harriet assured him.

'I wish I had found the family.'

Slowly he led her among the graves. He was widowed, Harriet thought; there were all the signs of that. On his own in some shabby rectory, managing as best he could.

'She left a few books behind,' he said. 'Her clothes were given to charities, but the books were left. I said I'd take them: we have a book sale every autumn.'

The coffin was being removed from the church. Harriet knew this was why she had been led away. No voices reached them where they walked. A door of whatever vehicle was there closed softly and then another one did.

* * *

Summer that year was fine and warm, September began well then was wet, October cold. In late November Harriet gave a party to celebrate Stephen's twenty-sixth birthday. Afterwards, in the early hours of the next day when everyone had gone, she and Stephen restored the rooms which more than a hundred people had disordered. Doing so, they talked about their guests, most of them of Stephen's generation; and in the kitchen Harriet washed up cutlery and glasses, Stephen dried and put away. They were in the drawing room again, plumping up cushions, finding what they had overlooked, when Stephen said, 'Do you remember Emily Vance? One of your cleaners?'

In the months that had passed since the funeral there had hardly been a day when Emily Vance hadn't come into Harriet's thoughts. When the clergyman had led her into the graveyard, the first drops of a shower had begun to spatter the tombstones. He had been inadequate. He would always know he had been, he said, as, unseen by both of them, the unknown girl was taken from the church where she'd found peace. And Harriet then had felt inadequate too.

The fire in the drawing room had long ago died down, but even so she put the fireguard in place. They should go to bed now. There wasn't much of the night left.

'When you were out we often were alone, Emily Vance and I,' Stephen said.

The stem of a glass had broken off, and Harriet watched him feeling where it had fallen for the dampness that would become a stain on the carpet. Finding nothing, he said the glass must have been empty.

'She thought it was kind of you to let her have her coffee in the garden when it was fine. Sometimes I had mine there too. She was a lonely person.'

In the kitchen he dropped the broken glass into the waste-bucket beneath the sink. Empty bottles crowded the draining boards. A blue cardigan, left behind by someone, was draped over the back of a chair.

'She doesn't know the names of flowers,' Stephen said. 'Not a single one. We walked about the garden and she would ask and I would tell.'

Harriet said they had done enough for one night and ran the hot water in the sink, brushing it round the sides to leave it clean. In the hall there was a scarf they hadn't noticed on the floor, left behind too. The telephone was off the hook. Stephen put it on again.

'Emily Vance died,' Harriet said on the stairs, because it had to be said now. 'I should have told you. I'm sorry.'

Stephen shook his head. He asked about the death and didn't flinch when he was told, was not surprised. 'She talked to me a bit,' he said. 'Not that it was easy for Emily Vance to talk to anyone.'

'She loved you.'

Stephen opened his bedroom door, turned on the light. It was a room that never changed. What was there he had chosen carefully, had taken nothing away, had added nothing. He was like that, which Harriet knew and he did not.

Standing with him in the open doorway, she heard a denial of what she had said. His voice was empty of emotion, as if already he was a consultant in a hospital. A child ran off from fear. A father promised. An acquiescent mother promised too. But still the child ran off, to search for strength in her concealment of herself, not ever to return, not ever to be found.

'She said it in the garden, in the matter-of-fact way of someone who cleans your house for you. She listened to my optimism: that all this was over for ever now. We spoke of love. She smiled a little, her gentle, lonely smile. She did not say, yet it was said, that in the rooms of a quiet house when she tried to love she could not love, and when she tried to hope she could not hope. We walked together, silent in the garden, and then she went away.'

* * *

In her bedroom, sitting by a window that overlooked the garden, Harriet wished she didn't know. She wished that what she had dreaded had happened instead, ordinary and understandable.

The last of night clung on, a misty light not yet enough to bring back shape and colour. The pear trees' blossom was elusive, tulips not their stately selves, aquilegia not there at all. Sunshine in its time would rescue ceanothus, and lilac in its corner, wallflowers and doronicum.

Shadows moved, not in the garden, three people, one a child. The rooms of a house were comfortable and unassuming, books in a bookcase, a telephone in the hall. Food was cooked and eaten, cleanness everywhere, and warmth. 'What use is anger?' Stephen had murmured as he closed his bedroom door, his professionalism at last affected by the distress that now was shared. Between the childhood and the death there was a life that hadn't been worth living.

The scarlet tinge of early peonies came suddenly, broom's yellow brightness, pink clematis, rosemary thriving. A chaffinch perched and waited. A blackbird looked about.

Harriet wept, and through the blur of her tears the beauty that had spread in her garden, and was spreading still, was lost in distortion. She watched it returning, becoming again resplendent, more even than it had been. But in a world that was all wrong it seemed this morning to be a mockery.

Making Conversation

'Yes?' Olivia says on the answering system when the doorbell rings in the middle of *The Return of the Thin Man*. The summons is an irritation on a Sunday afternoon, when it couldn't possibly be the meter-man or the postman, and it's most unlikely to be Courtney Haynes, the porter.

A woman's voice crackles back at her but Olivia can't hear what she says. More distinctly, the dialogue of the film reaches her from the sitting room. 'Cocktail time,' William Powell is saying, and there's the barking of a dog. The man Olivia lives with laughs.

'I'm sorry,' Olivia says in the hall. 'I can't quite hear you.'

'I'm not used to these answering gadgets.' The woman's voice is clearer now. There is a pause, and then: 'Is my husband there?'

'Your *husband*?' Frowning, more irritated than she has been, Olivia suggests the wrong bell has been rung.

'Oh, no,' the voice insists. 'Oh, no.'

'I really do think so. This is number 19.'

Dark-haired, dark-eyed, with a crushed quality about her features that doesn't detract from their beauty, Olivia at thirty-seven has been separated from her husband for years and feels the better for it. She has chosen not to marry the man she lives with; there is a feeling of independence about her life now, which she likes.

'I've come up from Brighton,' the woman two flights below states. 'I'm Mrs Vinnicombe.'

* * *

Olivia met Vinnicombe on the street. She tripped as she was leaving a house in Hill Street – number 17 – where she had just been interviewed for a job she particularly wanted. She lost her balance, stumbled down two steps and fell on to the pavement, her handbag scattering its contents, her left knee grazed, tights badly torn. Vinnicombe was passing.

He helped her to her feet, collected her belongings together, noticed her grimace of pain when she began to hobble off after she'd thanked him. 'No, no, you're shaken,' he said, and insisted that she sat for a while in the saloon bar at the end of the street. He bought her brandy, although she didn't ask for it.

He was an overweight man in a dark suit that needed pressing, Olivia noticed when she had pulled herself together. He was probably forty-two or -three, his pigeon-coloured hair thinning at the temples, a tendency to pastiness in his complexion. Feeling foolish and embarrassed, hoping that the incident hadn't been observed from the house where she'd been interviewed, Olivia insisted that she was perfectly all right now. 'You'll get the job,' the man assured her when she told him why she was in Hill Street. He spoke with such certainty that she thought for a moment he was himself connected with the offices she had visited and had some influence there. But this turned out not to be so. The colour had come back into her cheeks, he said. No one would not give her a job, he said.

This confidence was well placed. A month later Olivia began work at number 17, and in time even told the people who had interviewed her how nervous she had been in case, glancing from a window, one of them had seen her sprawled all over the pavement. She laughed about it, and so did they. 'I was rescued,' she explained in the same light-hearted way, 'by a gallant passer-by.' Sometimes, when telling other people in the office about the incident, she jestingly called her rescuer a guardian angel. She remembered only that the man had been of unprepossessing appearance, that he had lightly held her elbow when she was on her feet again, and that his voice had warned her she'd been shaken. It was winter then, a January day when she stumbled down the steps, 14 February when she began to work for her new employers. In April, when the window-box daffodils were in bloom, a man smiled shyly at her in Hill Street, and for a moment, as she walked past, Olivia couldn't remember where she had seen that podgy face before. 'You got the job,' a voice – hardly raised – called after her.

'Oh, goodness, I'm sorry!' Olivia cried, ashamed and turning round. She almost exclaimed, 'My guardian angel!' It would have pleased him, she knew. You could guess it would, even on so slight an acquaintance.

'You're well?' he asked. 'You like it in there?' He gestured at the offices she had just left, and Olivia said, yes, she did. He walked with her to the corner and they parted there.

Then, one lunchtime, less than a week later, he was in Zampoli's in Shepherd Market and asked if he might share her table. He asked her name when he had ordered steak-and-kidney and she a chicken salad. His was Vinnicombe, he said. 'Oh, I invent things,' he answered when, making conversation, she enquired; and Olivia thought of Edison and Stephenson and Leonardo da Vinci, of the motor-car and the aeroplane and space travel.

But Vinnicombe's inventions were not like that. His were domestic gadgets and accessories: fasteners for electric and gas ovens, for microwave ovens, for refrigerators and deep-freezes. He had invented a twin eggcup, a different kind of potato peeler, a carousel for drip-drying purposes, an electronic spike for opening and closing windows, a folding coat-hanger, a TV-dinner aid. Olivia tried to be interested.

* * *

'He isn't here,' his wife says, agitated. In Olivia's sitting room the television screen is blank and soundless now. The man she lives with, annoyed that it has to be so because of a visitor, is having a bath. A Sunday newspaper has been tidied up a bit, a chair pushed back.

'Of course your husband isn't here, Mrs Vinnicombe.'

She shouldn't have let her in, Olivia is thinking. This woman has no possible right in the flat, no right to disturb their weekend peace. And yet when Mrs Vinnicombe said who she was, Olivia had found it hard to shout into the house telephone that she did not intend to allow her admittance.

'I thought he might be here.' Olivia's visitor eyes the scarlet blooms of an amaryllis in a plain white container. She is a tall woman, big-boned, with henna-dyed hair, her bright fingernails the same shade as the lipstick that increases by a millimetre or so the natural outline of her lips.

'I thought I'd better come.' Specks of pink have appeared in Mrs Vinnicombe's gaunt cheeks, confirming her agitation. It's difficult for her, Olivia tells herself, and does not attempt to make it easier. She sits down also, and is silent.

* * *

A week after their second encounter Vinnicombe telephoned Olivia, knowing now where she worked. He invited her to have a drink one evening, a proposition that caused her some embarrassment. This man had been kind to her on the street; it had seemed natural that he should ask to share her table in a crowded lunchtime restaurant; but telephoning the office, issuing a specific invitation, was different. 'Oh, really, it's very kind,' she said, trying to leave it at that.

'You asked me about kitchen extractors,' he reminded her on the telephone and she remembered that, again making conversation, she had. 'I've got a couple of brochures for you. I'd just like to pass them over.'

And so they met again, not in the saloon bar where he had taken her after the incident on the street but in one that was further away. It was he who suggested that, and afterwards Olivia wondered if he'd made the choice because people from her office didn't frequent this bar, if he guessed that their tête-à-tête might possibly be a source of awkwardness for her. He had acquired three brochures for kitchen extractors. One of them he particularly recommended. Olivia was between love affairs then, temporarily on her own,

which she believed this man had somehow sensed;
she had certainly never said so.

'I'd put it in for you,' he offered. 'No problem, that.'

'Oh, heavens, no.'

'You'd save a tidy bit.'

'I couldn't possibly let you.'

It wouldn't take more than an hour or two, he said,
one Saturday morning. He laughed, displaying small,
evenly arranged teeth. 'My stock in trade.'

'Oh, no, no. Thanks all the same.'

His eyes were the feature you noticed: softly brown,
they had a moist look, suggesting a residue of tears,
and yet were not quite sad. It was more sentiment than
sorrow that distinguished them, and what seemed
like vulnerability. He could acquire any of the three
extractors at trade terms, but the reduction for the
recommended one was greater. Some cowboy could
easily make a botched job of the installation, dozens
of times he'd known it to happen.

'I'll think about it all,' Olivia promised, and afterwards on the Underground she found herself wondering
if he was lonely. He hadn't mentioned anything about
his private life except that he lived in Brighton and
always had.

'If you're interested in that particular model,' he
said on the phone two days later, 'there's one that's
ordered and the lady's seemingly changed her mind.
In black, as you said you wanted. So there'd be a

reduction on the price I gave you, not that there's anything wrong with it, not even shop-soiled.'

Since Olivia did need an extractor in her small kitchen, it seemed silly to reject this bargain offer. She
began to say again that she couldn't possibly allow
Vinnicombe to install it for her, but already he was
insisting, reminding her of this further saving if he
did. It seemed rude to go on refusing what he offered,
especially as he had already gone to the trouble of
finding out so much.

'I'd really rather . . .' she began, making one last
effort, then giving in.

∗　　∗　　∗

At Olivia's invitation Mrs Vinnicombe has settled
herself uneasily on the pale cushions of the sofa but,
as if she fears to do so, she does not come to the point.
She mentions Brighton again, as conversationally as
her husband did when he said he had always lived
there. She describes the waves splashing against the
pier and the concrete walls of the promenade. She
was married in Brighton, she says; a mortgage was
taken out locally on the house she has lived in since
that time. Her two boys were born not five hundred
yards from that house, the younger one – Kevin – the
last infant to be delivered in the old maternity home,
now the site of a petrol station. As a child herself,
she built sandcastles when the sea was far enough

out; her back and arms peeled one summer, not covered in time.

'Of course, he told me about you,' she eventually brings herself to say. 'Well, naturally, you know that.'

'Told you what, Mrs Vinnicombe?'

Mrs Vinnicombe slightly shakes her head, as if an exactitude here is not important, as if what she has said is enough.

'Sixteen Kevin is now, Josh two years older. Well, of course, you know that too. I'm sorry.'

'Why have you come here, Mrs Vinnicombe?'

The specks of pink have spread in the gaunt cheeks and are blotches now. A trace of lipstick has found its way on to one of Mrs Vinnicombe's front teeth. She looks away, her gaze again settling on the exotic amaryllis.

'You took my husband from me. I came to get him back.'

*   *   *

The installing of the extractor lasted longer than a couple of hours. They had lunch together at the kitchen table, soup and salad and the Milleens cheese Olivia had bought the day before. 'Just a minute,' Vinnicombe said at one point and went out, returning with Danish pastries. Later, when he finished just before six, Olivia offered him a drink. She opened a bottle of Beaune and they sat in the sitting room.

'Thank you,' he said when they had finished the wine, when eventually he stood up to go.

'I'm awfully grateful,' she said, realizing as she spoke that he had been going to say something else, that unintentionally she had interrupted him.

'It's been so nice,' he said. 'Today has been so nice.'

She smiled, not knowing how to respond. She felt nervous again, as she had the first time he telephoned the office. She wrote a cheque. He folded it into his wallet. He had been adamant about not charging for his labour.

'What'll you do, Olivia?' he asked, for the first time using her Christian name. 'How'll you spend what's left of today?'

And she said, wash her hair, because that was true, and watch something on television, and read in bed. She hardly ever went out on Saturday nights, she said.

'I have to tell you something,' he said. 'That first day when we met: remember that day, Olivia?'

'Yes, of course.'

'I fell in love with you that day, Olivia.'

He was looking straight at her when he said that, his moist brown eyes steadily fixed on hers. Once or twice before, Olivia had met their stare and had been aware of something that reminded her of pleading, as from a child.

'I had to tell you,' he said.

She shook her head, smiling, endeavouring to

register that she was flattered yet also that what was said must surely be an exaggeration. Olivia had quite often been told before that she was loved and had felt flattered on each occasion; but this was different because, somehow, it was all absurd.

'I don't suppose,' he said, 'we could meet again?'

'No, I don't think that's a good idea.'

'I had to tell you.'

He had brought a metal tool-container with him and he picked this up from beside the kitchen door. He offered to take away the carton and the packing the extractor had come in, but she said that wasn't necessary, that she could easily dispose of them. He took them all the same, for the third time saying that he had had to tell her.

*　*　*

'I was twenty when we married,' Mrs Vinnicombe says. 'I'm forty-one now. It's quite a time, you know. The boys growing up; months there were with not a penny coming into the house. Oh, it's better now. I'm not saying for an instant it isn't better in that respect. Not well off, not even comfortable sometimes, but near enough to not having to worry. It's been a partnership, you know: I've always done the invoicing and accounts, the tax returns, the VAT. Not that I'm trained: I worked in Hazlitt's, the jeweller's. That's where he found me.'

'Mrs Vinnicombe, you've got the wrong end of the stick. By the sound of what you're saying, you're under a very considerable misapprehension.'

Mrs Vinnicombe shakes her head in her dismissive manner, a tiny movement, not one of impatience. Then, as if she has in some way been unfair or discourteous, she says that when her husband told her he held nothing back. Long before that, though, she knew that something was wrong.

'Well, any woman would. And the boys – well, I've watched the boys becoming frightened. There's no other word for it. I've watched him ceasing to be bothered with them.'

'I didn't take your husband from you, Mrs Vinnicombe. That is totally untrue. As you can see, I'm perfectly happily –'

'He gave me the address, no argument at all when I asked him where you lived. Oh, ages ago that was. I don't know why I asked him. I never thought I'd come here.'

'Please listen to me, Mrs Vinnicombe.'

After the Saturday of the extractor installation, Vinnicombe became a nuisance. When he'd said he had to tell her, when he'd asked if they might meet again and she'd said no, he hadn't passed out of her life, as she imagined he would. He telephoned on the Monday and before he could say anything she thanked him for his work in her kitchen. 'Just one quick drink,' he pleaded, and she repeated, even more firmly than she already had, that what he was suggesting was not a good idea. When he pressed her, she said she was sorry if she had ever given him reason to suppose that a relationship such as he was proposing was possible. He took no notice, he didn't appear to hear. 'No more than ten minutes,' he said. 'Ten minutes.'

Olivia places these facts before Mrs Vinnicombe, speaking slowly and carefully. She is anxious to arrange every detail exactly where it belongs, to ensure that Mrs Vinnicombe perfectly understands.

* * *

'Look, it's an intrusion,' Olivia said when he was there on the street again, less than a week after his Monday telephone call. He only wanted to explain, he said. 'That's all, and then it's over.'

So reluctantly, and saying she was reluctant, she met him again, in the bar that was not frequented by her office colleagues. 'I can't help loving you,' he said even before their drinks were ordered. 'From the very first moment I haven't been able to help it.'

He told her then all that Mrs Vinnicombe has repeated: about their house and their children. He had no affection for his wife. Once he had, there was none left now: for fourteen years he had been indifferent to her. Quite out of the blue, astonishing Olivia, he mentioned New Zealand, promising she would be happy with him there. He said he had connections in New Zealand.

'All this is silly. I'm practically a stranger to you.'

He shook his head and smiled. 'I lie awake at night and every word you've spoken to me returns. In passing once, our fingers touched. When you fell down I could have taken you in my arms. Even then I wanted to. I can still feel your elbow in the palm of my left hand. I never loved anyone before. Never.'

His eyes were luminous in his pasty face, a tug that might have been a threat of tears worked at the corners of his mouth. He would do anything, he said, he would take on any work to buy her things she wanted. In New Zealand, he said, they would build a life together.

'I must go now,' Olivia said, and walked away from him.

Again, one lunchtime, he was in Zampoli's; she didn't go there after that. He wrote long letters that were incoherent in places. They described Olivia's beauty, the way she smiled, the way she stood, the way she spoke. He would know everything one day, they said: as much as she could remember herself about her childhood and her dreams. She would tell him her dreams at breakfast-time; they would sit in the sun when they were old. She tore the letters up, but sometimes he was there on the street when she looked from the windows of her flat or from the window of her office. She took to leaving the office by going through the garages at the back, into the mews. On the telephone she didn't speak when she heard his voice.

Once, at the cinema on her own, he arrived in the seat next to hers, and when she moved away he followed her. 'I'm sorry,' he said on the street when she had to leave. Furious, Olivia threatened to make a complaint if that ever occurred again. Unless he left her in peace she would consider asking the police for advice.

'I love you, Olivia.'

'What you're doing amounts to harassment. You have no right –'

'No, I have no right.'

But Olivia knew she could not bring herself to go to the police, nor even to complain to a cinema manager. One evening he was on the Tube with her and spoke to her as if they'd met by chance. He was there again, behind her on the moving staircase, and at the ticket barrier. 'Oh, all right,' she wearily agreed when he invited her to have a drink, hoping in her frustration that if she went through everything she had already said he would at last be affected, would at last see the absurdity of the situation he had created.

They sat beside one another on a red-upholstered banquette and again there was the pleading in his eyes, and suddenly Olivia felt sorry for him. Seven months had passed since he had looked after her on the street. He was a man in torment was what she thought, a man doing his best to talk about other matters, to tell her about an apple-corer he had just interested a manufacturer in. As she had not before, she wondered about his wife, about the house in Brighton he returned to, about his boys. 'Did you always invent things?' she heard herself asking, and for the first time a connection was made with a period of her life that still inspired resentment if she brooded on it. When she was fifteen, when she was lumbering through that gawky time, there was her sister's friend, fiancé as he became, husband in the end. In the hall she had reached up to feel the peak of his military cap, to run a finger round the leather band that touched his hair. And for a passing moment, as she sat on that red banquette with a man who was a nuisance, Olivia felt again the pain there'd been.

* * *

Music comes faintly from the bathroom: the end of the first movement of Mahler's First Symphony. Then a tap is turned on and the music is drowned.

'Your husband's only been here once, Mrs Vinnicombe. To fit an extractor over my electric hob.'

Olivia doesn't reveal to Mrs Vinnicombe that her husband said he was indifferent to her, or proposed a new life in New Zealand with a stranger. Instead she asks if what Mrs Vinnicombe is saying is that she doesn't know where her husband is.

'My hope was he'd be here.'

'Your *hope*?'

'He only wanted to be with you. No bones about it: he said he couldn't lie. A meaning in his life. He used those words.'

Mrs Vinnicombe is talkative now. Her unease has dissipated; fingers twisting into one another a moment ago are still.

'He never made me think you were a go-getting woman. I never thought of you as that. "Don't blame her," he said, no more than two days ago, but then he'd said it already. When he told me was the time he said it first, and often after that.' Her voice is flat, empty of emotion. She says she's frightened. She says again her hope had been to find her husband here.

'I don't think I understand that, Mrs Vinnicombe.'

'He took nothing with him. No shaving things, pyjamas. He didn't say goodbye.'

How long, Olivia begins to ask, and is immediately interrupted.

'Oh, just since yesterday.'

'Your husband and I were not having any kind of love affair.' She gave him no encouragement, Olivia says: not once has she done that. She doesn't say she pitied him after he followed her from the Tube station, the night they sat together on the red-upholstered banquette, the night she asked him if he had always invented things. These details, now, seem neither here nor there: omitting to relate them is not intended to mislead. 'Why don't we have a bite to eat?' he said and, still pitying, she allowed him to take her to a place he knew nearby, called the Chunky Chicken Platter. 'All right for you?' he solicitously enquired when they were given a table there, and it was then that she knew she was pitying herself as well. A Good Friday it had been when she reached up in the hall to touch the cap of the man her sister was to marry. A Sunday, weeks later, when she lifted it down and pressed it to her face.

'Your husband wasn't even a friend, Mrs Vinnicombe.'

Hearing that, Olivia's visitor looks away, her head a little bent. How can that be, she softly asks, since he has done odd jobs about the place? How can it be, since he has described a woman's hair and her eyes, the way she stands, her voice, her slender legs, her neck, her hands?

'I was sick,' Mrs Vinnicombe adds to all this. 'I got up one night, three o'clock in the morning. I couldn't sleep, I vomited in the bathroom. Your stomach turns over with jealousy, hour after hour, and then you're sick. I didn't tell him. Well, naturally.'

'You have no cause for jealousy, Mrs Vinnicombe.' Olivia begins at the beginning, from the moment on the street to meeting Vinnicombe again, by chance, she thought; and his being, by chance also it seemed, in Zampoli's that day; how after that he bothered her. She can think of no other way to put it, even though it sounds a harsh way of describing the attentions of a man whose wife is in distress. The chicken place he took her to was horrible.

'Oh, jealousy is vile, I grant you that.' And as if Olivia hasn't offered a single word of explanation, Mrs Vinnicombe pursues the thread of her conviction. 'Yet there it is, and nothing you can do. I always knew when he'd been with you. Oh, not smears of lipstick, tell-tale perfume – nothing like that. It was worse because he wasn't the kind of man to have a woman, not the kind you read about in the papers. He wouldn't have made the papers in a million years. He took the boys out with their kites when they were little. He brought cakes back, treats for tea, always something when he had a bit to spare. They'll miss that now. They'll think of it when they think of him.'

'Mrs Vinnicombe, you can see your husband isn't here. I've been living here with someone else for months. I've no idea where your husband is.'

'I came to plead with you and with him too, to talk about the boys. I came to say to him we were a family.'

Mrs Vinnicombe's tears, so long held back, come now. She weeps on Olivia's sofa and her tears run through her make-up, smearing it. Her weeping drags at the contours of her face, bunching the flesh into ugly grimaces. She tries to speak and cannot. She doesn't search in her handbag for a tissue or a handkerchief but sits there, stark and upright on the pale cushions, noisily sobbing as she might in private.

'"Oh, God, let him be there" was what I asked when I rang your bell.'

'I don't understand what you're saying, Mrs Vinnicombe.'

But Olivia does. Her protest is conventional, all she can think of to say. She doesn't want to share her visitor's thoughts. None of it concerns her.

'You took my husband.'

Abruptly, Mrs Vinnicombe rises.

'You took my husband and now you can't give him back to me.' She crosses the room to the hall, not answering questions that are put to her. 'I keep on seeing him,' she says, 'and his footsteps on the sand. On soft, wet sand and then they ooze away to nothing.'

She does not speak again. Some minutes later Olivia sees her from a window, crossing the empty Sunday street, walking slowly, as if the encounter has drained her energy. She passes from view, slipping round the corner.

'I hear you're learning German.' Her sister's friend smiled. 'I like your dress,' he said, and her sister said that dress had been one of hers. He went on talking when her sister wasn't there. He knew of course: making conversation was a kindness offered.

Mahler is still playing in the bathroom, just audible above the sound of water running out. The day her sister married, Olivia looked down at her bedside lamp and whispered to herself that all she had to do was to press the bulb out and place her thumb, dampened with spit, in the socket. That day she saw her coffin carried, lowered while he stood at the graveside, the collar of his overcoat turned up. She heard her own voice murmuring from a romantic shroud, 'My darling, I have loved you so.'

Olivia gazes from the window at pigeons waddling beneath a tree. Raindrops spatter the pavement, then rain falls heavily and the pigeons crossly flutter off, in search of shelter. His wife is on the train by now, huddled in her corner, pretending to watch the houses going by, the same rain falling. Somewhere else, maybe, it falls for him. The balance of the mind disturbed: the woman on her train wonders if that worn expression will soon be used. He, wherever he is, already knows better.

He'll be there when she returns – or tomorrow or the next day – and in their house in Brighton they'll tack together a marriage and the family life his foolishness spoilt. He'll hear her repeating many times that she saw his footsteps disappearing on soft, wet sand. He'll not confess that he, too, imagined his last thoughts reaching out towards his hopeless love, that he imagined the seaweed in his clothes, and sand beneath his eyelids and in his mouth. He'll not confess he knew, in the end, that the drama of death does not come into it – that some pain's too dull to be worthy of a romantic shroud. Courage could have brushed glamour over what little there was, but courage is ridiculous when the other person doesn't want to know.

Giotto's Angels

On a stretch of pavement between Truman's Corner and Buswell's Hotel a man asked a child if she knew where St Ardo's was. The child passed the query on to another child, causing both of them to giggle.

'Don't worry about it,' the man said, smiling at the children who at once ran away, having been warned about men who smiled. An African woman who was passing was asked the same question and said there was a St Joseph's out Springfield way. The man said it didn't matter.

He was a man of forty-one with finely chiselled features, red-brown hair and Wedgwood-blue eyes that had once been alert but were not now. They hadn't been since a bright May morning in 2001 when he had found himself on a seat in one of the city parks feeling as if he had just woken up. Bewildered, he had wanted only to remain where he'd found himself, but later in the day a park keeper became concerned about him and summoned an ambulance. In the hospital he was taken to it was discovered that he could read and write. An amnesic abnormality was diagnosed, and when repeatedly the man was asked his name he was silent at first then answered in a garbled manner that was not understood. When he was searched his pockets were empty. No wallet was found, no scraps of paper, no name-tapes on his clothes, no information of any kind about himself. He was thought to be a house-painter, but the only evidence for this was traces of paint beneath his fingernails; no paint was found on his shirt-cuffs nor anywhere on his clothes or shoes. He remained in the hospital's care for several days until one early morning he dressed himself and, unnoticed, went away.

He was a picture-restorer by profession, and often seemed unusual, even strange, to other people, for his erratic memory caused him to rely on conjecture and deduction. When privately he considered his life – as much of it as he knew – it seemed to be a thing of unrelated shreds and blurs, something not unlike the damaged canvases that were brought to him for attention. His name was Constantine Naylor. He had forgotten that it was and wondered sometimes why that name came into his head. He liked it and tried to keep it there, but could not.

That day he searched the city for St Ardo's, not knowing what he was looking for nor why the two words were in his head. Outside the College of Surgeons he sought help from a bearded man and the man told him to clear off. He looked at a name written up, white letters on blue, Harcourt St. The familiarity of the two colours, the oblong shape of the metal sign, reassured him. Nailed into the brick that sign would be, he said to himself, and it was the same thing when he went on: Hatch St, Upr Charlemont St, North-brook, Ranelagh Rd. 'Nowhere here what you're looking for,' a man sponging water on a shop window told him.

'Never was,' a postman said.

There was a key in one of his pockets but he didn't know why it was there or what it was to. He came to a church and he stood outside it for a few minutes, read-ing the information on the black board by the gate. A memory came to him in the way it sometimes did, emerging from nowhere but very clear, and he knew the voice when he heard it in his mind. 'I'm asking you, boy, give us the counties of Ulster. Say the coun-ties off for us, Broderick, get up on your feet now.' And Broderick did, his awful old muffler half in rags and Mr Jameson said take that thing off. Mr Jameson was a drinker, he came out of O'Daly's footless and if he'd see you he'd go back in. 'Well, bedad, Broderick, you'll have me crucified,' he said when Broderick was silent, not knowing the counties. 'Donegal, Derry, Antrim, Down,' Mr Jameson prompted, but the prompt was no help to poor Broderick. Then the memory slithered away and there was nothing.

Appian Way was written up, Morehampton Rd. Dogs were being walked, five of them together on strings. 'Don't be long out,' Kitty said. 'Don't let the terrier off the lead till you'd come to the field.' They bought the terrier from Dwyer in Shannon's, who bred them. He could remember that well and he tried to hold on to it, Dwyer's long, long face and the terrier picked out for the looks of it, but he couldn't hold it. Slippery like some old snake it was.

All day he went about, was hungry, had peas and mash with a sausage and was brought a glass of cordial, pale pink, without a taste. He examined the photographs outside the Corinthian Cinema, crossed over into Hawkins Street and stood in a doorway. He waited for the dark and went slowly when he walked on. There was nothing in his mind except what he was looking for, the name carved on a pillar, and gates. In the evening usually there'd be nothing.

The lamps along the street were lit. Colours flashed in the sky, advertisements for drink or food, BOVRIL. He gave a coin to a musician with a melodeon. He took out what was left in his trouser pockets to count it. Silver in one pocket, coppers in the other was how he carried his money. He'd be all right with what he had, he said to himself, but to be sure he took the money out again and looked at the silver in the palm of his hand.

He went on then, asking no one in case it would give offence when people were in a hurry. In a public house he took a glass of beer to an empty corner and sat there for a long while. The bar was full of drinkers when he went in and he watched it emptying. A woman in the doorway spoke to him when he was on the street again. 'Short time?' she said.

Her lipstick glistened in the street light. Her black hair was thick and curled, the red coat she wore open. Her blouse had the tired look of a garment worn too long, its top buttons undone or missing. She smelt of perfume and cigarettes.

'I see you often,' she said.

He shook his head. Maybe someone else, he said. He'd got out of his way, trying all day to find St Ardo's, he said. He didn't know these parts at all.

The woman eyed him blankly, not saying anything. Her face was heavy, her eyes calculating, but otherwise uninterested. He asked her if she knew St Ardo's at all and she didn't answer. She said would they go over to Liffey Lane.

He felt for the key in his pocket, wanting to take it out and look at it because sometimes if you did a memory would come out of the fogginess of nothing. But he didn't in case the woman would think he was peculiar, looking at a key.

'I seen you all right,' she said. 'One o'clock in the morning and you'd be walking the streets.' There was a scaffold up in Liffey Lane, she said, and a shed left open. 'Would we go there?' she suggested.

He shook his head again. He said he wasn't looking for Liffey Lane. Not anywhere like that at all.

'Ah, you are, you are.'

She reached for his arm and took it, pressing it under hers. The expression on her face, serious and intent, hadn't changed. She didn't smile.

'You're an educated man,' she said. 'You have that way with you.'

She held him tightly, her fingers clamping his arm just below the elbow. She pulled it a bit and he could feel the soft yield of a breast. 'You're a fine man,' she whispered, a hoarseness coming into her voice. 'I couldn't go with some of them.'

They passed into a quay and turned out of it almost at once, leaving what traffic there was behind. A siren sounded, coming from far away. No one else was about. Five minutes, the woman had said, but twenty or twenty-five passed before they reached Liffey Lane and they still went on. 'There's no one only myself comes over here,' she said.

He knew where he was. That came suddenly, in the way that knowing anything did. The woman was pressing herself closer to him but he didn't care what she did. He didn't listen when she talked again about where they were going, telling him they'd be quiet there. He felt for the key again to make sure it was there and it was.

'I was confused,' he said. 'I have a groggy memory.'

* * *

She wondered if he was mad. Often you'd be with a man and you'd think he wasn't the full shilling, the attentions he'd ask for in a workman's shed and the way he'd be giving you talk you wouldn't want to hear. She mentioned money, saying the amount but he didn't comment on that. He didn't say he hadn't that much on him the way they usually did, looking for a reduction. He was pointing at a warehouse and the next minute at another one. 'God, it'll be great,' she said, making an effort to keep the conversation going.

Denise, her name was. She'd been a dressmaker and had gone on the streets because she preferred the work and earned more there. Fifteen years ago she'd lost touch with the husband she'd married when she was young. She was older than she looked.

* * *

It had happened before that he couldn't remember where he lived. He didn't know it had. He didn't know that when he was distressed St Ardo's came into his mind, that he clung to it because there was nothing else to cling to, although he didn't know where, or what, St Ardo's was. 'What's your name?' he asked the woman he was with, and she told him. She hadn't been born Denise, she said. 'A terrible name they give me.'

She didn't say what it was. He didn't ask. Something would be wrong, he thought. Many's the time you'd think it'd be all right and it wouldn't.

But when he tried the key it turned in the lock. He pushed the black door open with his shoulder.

* * *

She'd never gone to where a man lived before. What took place with a man did so outside mostly, or in the workman's shed or with luck in a car. Where she was now was a warehouse.

He turned a light on and she followed him. They passed through a big, empty void and up a stairs that was no more than a ladder. An attempt at domestic conversion had been begun and appeared to have been abandoned. 'You'd call me a caretaker,' he said.

He was different here, she thought, without the hint of the panic that had been in his manner and his voice before, nervous maybe, as often they were. She said the place was great. Convenient, she said.

Pipes were exposed, the roof beams rough, strengthened here and there with iron clamps, floor-boards unstained. Furniture was a bed, three wooden chairs, a table, a cupboard. Electric wires ran along the concrete of the walls, but there were pictures hanging there too, others stacked, one on a black-board easel.

'Well, isn't that great!' she said. 'Aren't you fixed rightly here!'

Often there were shadows or only fragments, echoes. A tall, sleek head was nodding now. Hands reached up to lift a picture from a wall. The red stones of a brooch were bright on a dark blouse, a man's voice saying, 'Skill like that, you should be your own master.' 'Wouldn't we fix him up with one of the warehouses?' the woman with the brooch said. 'Wouldn't he be better off?' It was the work that kept him going; he knew the work, he never made a mistake, not once, not ever. There was more to the work than the cleaning and you wouldn't see the extent of it until you'd taken off the smoke damage. The time he was in the grey house he restored sixteen canvases, and that was written down. Always write things down, they said, and he always did. The bell would ring, you'd take the same place you always took on the bench and it might be a mutton stew or fried fish and tomatoes or rissoles. Write everything down, only sometimes he'd forget. But the way it was, he'd never forget a picture.

'Would we take a beer?' the woman who'd come with him asked. 'Have you a beer at all?'

*　*　*

She wondered if he heard her, and then he turned around from looking at the picture he had on the easel. 'Giotto's angels,' he said.

She didn't understand, but when she went closer she could make out figures floating in the sky above mountain-side rocks. There was a single tree, its leaves all gone. You had to peer to make out what else there was, but when he showed her a coloured postcard of the picture it was easier. At first it didn't look the same and he explained that the angels were a copy of only a part of it, a crooked wall left out, and people in robes gathered round a dead body. He said the copy had been left in with him to see could he restore what had been lost in damp. He showed her what he had cleared already, a patch in the bottom right-hand corner. He filled a kettle at the sink and lit a gas stove. She mentioned the sum of money she had mentioned before.

'Ah no,' he said. 'Ah no.'

'What're you playing at, mister?'

He didn't say anything. He went back to the picture, dabbing it with a cloth. A smell was coming from the spirit he was using.

'You're misleading me the entire time,' she complained, but she didn't hurry him. You could get a man round no matter what the hold-up was. If you took it easy and let him find his own pace you could.

There were notes stuck all round the doorframe, scraps of paper attached with drawing-pins. There were picture postcards like the one he'd shown her attached to the door itself. An old suitcase was on the floor, the lid open, propped against an iron girder in the wall. Different-coloured paints had been tried out on it in daubs, and on the inside of it and on the girder and the floor. Brushes were in jars. Empty picture frames hung from nails in the walls.

There's money here, she thought.

* * *

He made tea when the kettle boiled. He said he was sorry if there'd been a misunderstanding. Because of his affliction, he explained, it was often like that. He looked in the cupboard for biscuits, but he must have had them all. He said he was sorry.

'No matter at all.' She came close to him, specks of spittle moistening his face when she spoke. On the streets he hadn't noticed that her lipstick was crooked, missing in places the outline of her lips and giving her a grotesque look.

'The only thing is,' she said, 'I'm at a loss on account of the misunderstanding.'

He gave her what money he had, two notes kept in an inside pocket, the coppers and the silver.

* * *

She counted what there was and watched him pouring tea for himself, a saucer under the cup. He didn't add anything to it, neither sugar nor milk. He sipped it and it would have been hot. She never touched tea, she said.

He worked at the picture again, his cup and saucer beside him on the floor. He'd given her more than she'd asked for on the street. She could finish the night because of that. But the bed looked comfortable. A double it was, better than what she had herself.

'Would you have another note,' she said, 'and I'll try for beer? Would there be somewhere open?'

He said there wouldn't. Maclin Street, O'Donohue's, he said, only they'd be closed up for the night.

He went to the scraps of paper on the doorframe and found the one he wanted. She thought he was looking for somewhere that might be open, but he wasn't. 'Knockmell,' he read out, and said he used to live in Knockmell. 'I have dreams it was a Knockmell woman showed me how you'd repair a picture. I lived a long time in Knockmell and they told me that's why I have a memory of it. I was told that and I wrote it down. I was a boy when I ran off from Knockmell. I did wrong, I don't know what it was.'

He had taken a paintbrush from his mouth in order to speak and he put it back, crossways between his teeth. He put paint on a smaller brush and touched the canvas with it in one place. He leant back to get a long view of the picture and then put a smear of paint on somewhere else.

'I have a bad leg,' she said.

She could feel it troublesome now. On her feet too long would bring that on, they'd told her. A lot could go wrong with a leg, they said, you'd never know what the trouble was. 'That's a great bed you have,' she said.

She went to the bed and lay down on it. He was back with his brushes again, not talking any more. She eased her shoes off and he paid no attention. It was a well-made bed, she could tell when she got into it, the blankets smooth over the sheets, the pillow soft.

The room was soundless now that he was silent. The clink of the cup on the saucer had ceased; the only movement was the paintbrush on the cleaned canvas, or the spirit being poured, the bottle corked again. The night noise of the city could not be heard and the stillness seemed like more of the bed's luxury. Beneath the covers she eased off her restricting garments.

She wasn't frightened. Often you would be with a man, but you couldn't be with this one, even though she didn't know where she was with him. Twice she'd had the money she'd been paid taken back from her when everything was over, the blade of a penknife shown to her, her arm twisted another time.

The quiet continued, the seated figure at work in no way disturbing it. She slept, though not intending to.

*   *   *

Baby angels he thought of them as, and he imagined music, maybe played by them, maybe not. Ten angels there were, and among the shadowy rocks there might have been others, lost now in time or rejected by Giotto's copyist. Not working for a moment, he examined the postcard and could see no more than the ten either. He tried to remember the name of the woman who'd left the painting in and when he couldn't he crossed the room to the door and found it: Mrs Sonia Maitland, address and telephone number given, her handwriting, not his. He would finish this picture tomorrow.

At the sink he washed the cup he had had his tea from. He dried it and dried the saucer. He washed his hands and brushed his teeth. He knelt to pray when he'd undressed and filled a glass of water for the night. His pyjamas were blue, striped with grey. He saw the woman lying there.

* * *

She woke and he was asleep beside her. A single electric bulb was lit, casting light on the picture of the angels, the darkness around it intense. She didn't know what time it was.

She lay there, content; he didn't stir. There would be money, she thought again, he would be paid for his work. There'd be a hiding place, notes of all denominations. He had no needs: accumulated, untouched, there would be money somewhere, forgotten.

She went about the room, not waking him, not putting on another light. She opened the cupboard and felt among his folded clothes, in pockets, at the back of each shelf. She opened tins and jars near where he'd made his tea, poked into sugar bags and cartons. She

looked among the stacked canvases, lifted down the
pictures from the walls, put everything back as tidily
as it had been. Even while he slept she felt beneath the
mattress. She looked for books, since notes were often
kept between the pages. There were no books. She
looked for drawers. There were none either. She took
a chance and turned another light on in order to
examine the floor. One of the boards was loose.

She extinguished the light she'd put on. With a kitchen knife she lifted the board easily. She propped it
open with one of her shoes, then lifted it higher and
saw the shadowy outline of something there. She
knew at once and reached in for a cardboard box. She
took the money, leaving none.

*　*　*

Denise drank with Bernie Reilly in Davin's. She didn't
say about last night, nor did she when Frances came
in. 'Well, Franco, how are you?' Bernie said, finishing
his glassful.

'God, he's a scut,' Frances said when he went away.

'Bring Franco a small one,' Denise called out to the
new lad behind the bar. 'And the same for myself.'

'Jeez, Den!' Franco exclaimed in mock disapproval
of whiskey being drunk so early in the day.

Denise laughed. She had counted the notes in the
Mercer Street toilets. It hadn't felt like theft and it hadn't
when she knew how much she'd taken. It didn't now.

'Are you in funds?' Frances asked her, but Denise didn't tell her although it would have made a tale all right, a man not laying a finger on her and angels in a picture lit up the whole night long, and the two of them asleep.

You couldn't forget it. You couldn't forget the conversation of the afflicted man, or how he was skilful with the brush and the paint, like a man brought back from the dead as soon as he had them by him. You couldn't forget the way he knew how to guide the little paintbrush into whatever part of the picture was defective and the colour coming then, how he'd do it without ever a hesitation.

'Wasn't it quiet last night, though?' Frances said. 'I packed it in early.'

'It was quiet all right.'

He was secure where he was, as if the emptiness around him protected him. You could feel that when you were there, all the time you could feel it. The way things were, she'd gone off in a hurry; she wished she hadn't. She could have fried him a bit of breakfast, a couple of rashers, whatever he'd have. She could have put out the knives and forks and sat down at the table with him. She'd sworn to God after the first time she went out on the streets that as long as she had breath in her she never would again, that she'd never again stand in the dark of a doorway, not wanting to be seen although being seen was what she was there for. Hours it had felt like when she waited in the half-quay the first time, and hours again before she felt up to walking back to the city streets, her clothes torn where the man she'd gone with had been rough.

'What's your hurry?' she said when Frances looked like she was going. 'Bring Franco another,' she called out to the new lad.

'Ah, no, Den,' Frances protested. She was on her feet, shaking her head at the boy, halfway to the door already. 'See ya, Den.'

'I had it poured,' the lad said, bringing what he had been asked for, and Denise paid for it.

No one else came in. She'd go back to the warehouse, Denise said to herself. It came to her suddenly that she would. She'd go back and give him the money he didn't know he had, or know he had ever possessed. A couple were in a corner, a man and his wife who came in every morning, who nodded at her sometimes but that was all. There was a bell-push beside the black door of the warehouse, a white little bell-push that stood out. You went through the emptiness, then up the ladder that was a stairs. 'Amn't I lucky?' was what he'd said and she could hear his voice echoing.

* * *

Mr Davin came in, to be ready early for the lunchtime custom. 'Good morning, Denise,' he greeted her. 'How ya doin'?'

'Great,' she said.

She'd buy bread and tins in a Quinsworth, she'd pour out Cairns for both of them. He'd be intent on his work and she'd get the board raised and the notes back under it. She'd make the bed if he hadn't done it, she'd sweep the floor over. 'Is that board there loose?' she'd ask and they'd raise it up together. She'd say, 'What's that?' and he'd look at what she was drawing his attention to. He'd reach in for it.

At the bar Mr Davin measured out another drink for her. She felt a twinge in her leg and sat down to rest it. She would go in when the door was opened for her and they would walk through the emptiness, as they had before. He would show her the picture as if he hadn't already. He wouldn't be surprised when she made the bed and swept the floor. He wouldn't know anything about her because she hadn't told him.

* * *

As she often did, Denise slept the afternoon away and woke at five. Still blurred from sleep, she let the day come back to her, and the notion that she'd return the money was the first thing she remembered. She'd been drunk in Davin's and Mr Davin said go home now. Keale from the barracks came in, the big smirk on his puss when he saw her and she said be careful and Mr Davin came over then. 'Don't give her another,' he instructed the new lad and the way he said it she wanted to show them the money. She had her bag open to take it out but then knew not to.

She took a spoonful of linctus to settle herself, she drank some water. A headache was beginning, like drumbeats behind her forehead. She lay down, and the notion she'd had in Davin's came over her again. She saw the angels, and the tip of the brush touching in the colours, and when he finished he came to her, the warmth of his body warming hers. 'Don't go from me,' he said.

She slept again, the headache still there when she woke at ten past seven. The money was in the Roses tin on top of the wardrobe where you couldn't see it. She'd been careless, opening her bag like that in Davin's. With drink in, she could have let some of the notes fall out, for the new lad or Keale to pick up later on with no one looking.

She stood on a chair and took down the Roses tin. Slowly, carefully, again she counted the money. All of it was there and she closed her eyes in relief, the beginning of a panic slipping away. Sitting on the edge of the bed, feeling better than she had, she shuffled the notes into a tidy stack, flattening turned-down corners, and pressing out creases as best she could. Returning them to the Roses tin, she noticed that one had fallen out and was lying on the bed. She picked it up and slipped it under her pillow, being short after the morning in Davin's.

She lay down with her eyes closed, her thoughts muddling on. That man was different from other men, she'd said to herself, and had felt when she was with him that she was different too. A misunderstanding had brought them together, her saviour, as she was his: that thought had come, and she remembered it. The drink talking was what it sounded like now.

Too long it was, the walk back to the warehouse, too long for a girl with a bad leg. She knew it wasn't and wondered why she lied to herself and why her courage, so briefly there, had deserted her. A distant longing nagged, too far away, elusive now. Her hand crept beneath the pillow; the note was good to touch. She watched the twilight shadows gathering, another night beginning.

* * *

He waited, not knowing why he did or what he waited for. Only the sounds he made himself disturbed the stillness of the night as he cleaned his brushes and put things ready for the morning. The paint had dried and when he turned the lights out, all but one, he looked again and saw perfection in his angels. There was no rustle in the quiet when he lay down, no fingers traced a way upon his flesh. He slept and waited still, but he knew in dreams that only angels were his solace.

An Idyll in Winter

Mary Bella didn't remember when she woke up and then she did: he hadn't come. The train was late and Woods had telephoned from the station. It was nearly ten by then and she must have fallen asleep waiting on the sofa. She didn't remember going up to bed.

It was very early now, she could tell by the light. The air coming in at the half-open window was cold and she pulled the bedclothes up. If he had come he would be in the room she had helped to get ready for him, the primroses she'd picked in the vase on the dressing-table. She wondered if he had.

When she slept again she dreamt he hadn't, that it was wrong about the train being late, that Woods came back alone and said a stranger hadn't got off that train. But when she went down to the breakfast room and listened at the door there was a voice she didn't know. 'Now why can I guess who this is!' he said when she went in, and held out his hand for her to shake. They had all summer, he said in the schoolroom after-wards. They had a lot to do.

It was she who called the nursery the schoolroom when she first had lessons there. Woods found a slate that might do for a blackboard, but it wasn't necessary since everything could be written in her different exercise books. Mary Bella was twelve that summer, thirteen when September came.

He wore blue jerseys, and blue shirts which her mother called Aertex, and tweed ties and whipcord trousers. Her mother said he reminded her of Leslie Howard in *Gone with the Wind*, her father that he was confident this chap would get her into Evelynscourt, which was the purpose of his being there. 'Enough for one morning,' he said every day when it was twelve o'clock, and they went about the farm then to see how things were getting on. Later in the afternoon they would ride to Worley Edge and sometimes on to Still Fell, or walk to Grattan's Tomb. 'Very Heathcliffian,' he said when there were riders racing one another on the moors, and she didn't understand what he meant. He read to her on their walks, or she to him, depending on what book it was. It made her sad that the summer had to end. He said it never would, because remembering wouldn't let it.

*   *   *

Anthony was twenty-two then and, not knowing what to do with himself after an undistinguished university career, he considered that a few months adding what he could to the education of a child in a country house would be better than doing nothing. The letter he received in reply to his answer to the advertisement was in an educated hand, and honestly laid out the disadvantages he would encounter if he took the post. *We are close to moorland, and remote. You may find the sense of solitude oppressive.* But the location turned out to be less intimidating than this suggested, the house – called Old Grange – grander than he had imagined, the farm prosperous.

Anthony delighted in the place as soon as he became familiar with it, and in Mary Bella too. Small for her age, sharp-witted and volatile, she smiled a lot and laughed a lot, the beginning of beauty already in her features, her manner touched with a child's unspoilt charm. In the schoolroom she disliked the dreariness of geography, and geometry's uninteresting straight lines and the silly shape of trapeziums. History caught her imagination, she learnt poetry easily, had a way with spelling and with words. And that summer, which was warm, with hardly any rain, she developed a fondness for Anthony that he could not dismiss or pretend he didn't notice and which, when September came, caused him more unease than he admitted to himself.

He left Old Grange the day after Mary Bella's thirteenth birthday, leaving behind far more than their excursions on the moors, their conversations, or the birds Mary Bella identified for him, far more than the hay-making he had helped with, or a family's friendliness. He left what he thought would be impossible to forget – the sadness Mary Bella had spoken of, and something like desperation in her eyes when the last day came and they said goodbye to one another. But Anthony did forget. He made himself, considering it better that he should.

*   *   *

Mary Bella passed, quite comfortably, the entrance examination for Evelynscourt, where her mother had been happy in her time but where Mary Bella wasn't. Too often and too easily she remembered the summer of the schoolroom, and nothing at Evelynscourt was like that. She didn't talk about the summer to anyone, not wanting to; and in the holidays she concealed her feelings every time she returned from riding to the places they had ridden to or when she sat alone in the schoolroom, the books of some holiday task or other spread out on the ink-stained table unheeded. She was reconciled to never seeing Anthony again, but his voice was there, as if it always would be, telling her about Jeanne d'Arc, and Elizabeth Tudor, whom he had called the Lonely Queen, and Charlemagne and Marie Antoinette. It drew her into the world of the Marshalsea, brought her to Dorlcote Mill and Wildfell Hall, made Haworth Parsonage as real as it had been.

*   *   *

Anthony became a cartographer, astonishing himself that he had not sooner been attracted by a profession that at once interested and absorbed him and in which, he discovered, he was both skilled and gifted. A few years after his months at Old Grange he had met at a party a slim, fair-haired girl called Nicola who, when they knew one another better, accompanied him on his commissions abroad. She took photographs for him in the uncharted region of the Abruzzi and in the new, mapless towns of Africa, in rebuilt Germany and where motorways now changed for ever the old roads of England. In time, they married. Two children – both girls – were born, a house acquired in the leafy London suburb of Barnes and, flourishing in contented motherhood and Anthony's devotion, Nicola's prettiness acquired a quiet confidence that had not been there before. Anthony went alone on his commissions and liked returning more than going away. Each time he came back, his children seemed a little different and another aspect of his small family was more than it had been before. His absences kept love alive, and interest in his children's pursuits did not wane as otherwise it might have. On Saturdays, if the week had been free of disobedience, there was a visit to Richmond Park, tea afterwards in the Maids of Honour. On Sundays Nicola's mother took the girls away for their day with her, returning them undamaged by excessive affection, for she was careful about that. How fortunate they all four were! Anthony often said, or Nicola did. Neither wondered how married life might have been if they had married other people, how different their children would be. It was enough to know that being married to one another was what they wanted, that neither wanted more. 'Tell them about Old Grange,' Nicola often urged, and Anthony would recall for the girls what he remembered of it. They always listened, as Nicola did too. Because it sounded so lovely, she said, and the girls agreed.

* * *

On the morning of her sixtieth birthday, Mary Bella's mother died, suddenly, without an illness' warning. Mary Bella was twenty-four then, had been at Old Grange since she'd left Evelynscourt, and was content to be there. She took her mother's place quite naturally, but in spite of the comfort and convenience of her presence her father was unable to come to terms with the tragedy that had so unexpectedly occurred. He did not ever recover his good humour or his affection for the house and the farm. In the darkness of his mood he took to drink a little and to riding recklessly over the moors as if in search of the happiness that had been taken from him. One day he did not come back and was later found after his horse returned alone. The fall was a bad one, but perhaps achieved for him what he wanted. He did not regain consciousness.

Mary Bella might have sold Old Grange, passed on to its new owner the horses and her small band of farm workers, the Charollais herd and several thousand sheep. Instead she remained, and often during the lonely months that followed her father's death she sat in the schoolroom as she had as a child, her sole companion a spaniel who, with age, had become blind. She knew she was living in the past, that the past would always be there, around her, that she was part of it herself.

*　　*　　*

It wasn't sentiment that in time brought Anthony back to the Yorkshire moors. By chance, his profession did, and when he found himself one morning not far from Worley Edge it was an impulse, stirred by curiosity, that caused him to park his car less than a mile from Old Grange. He walked then, skirting the walled garden and the farm buildings when he came to them. There was a silence about the place, a tranquillity quite at odds with the clatter of the yard, the hurrying and the bustle that had lived on in his recollections. Not knowing why he passed the house by, he followed a right-of-way he remembered.

The morning, in early April, was fine. Except for sheep, the moors were empty. No horses raced there, no solitary figure – a movement in the distance – climbed to Grattan's Tomb: going on, Anthony realized he had been expecting to see that. He remembered the places where they had rested on their walks, where he had read from *Wuthering Heights* or listened to another page of *The Chimes*, or where he had insisted that only French should be spoken.

He turned before he reached Still Fell. Carelessly selective, his memory had misled him. Only once had there been horses racing on the moors; it was unlikely that they would have been there today at this time, and long ago the child he had taught would surely have left so remote a house. He turned and walked back the way he had come, hesitated for a moment, and then passed between the avenue's two grey pillars.

The big, wide front door was as it always had been, sunburnt pale, in need again of paint. He went to the side entrance, a door without a knocker or a bell, bolted only at night. When he pushed it open the same picture – trapeze performers above a circus ring – still decorated one wall of the long, cold corridor that led to the kitchen and the sculleries. There was a murmur of voices, the rattle occasionally of a knife or fork put down. 'Hello,' Anthony called out, and his voice silenced everything.

In the kitchen the faces around the table were not at first familiar. Six or seven men, a slight, dark-haired woman in a blue dress, looked back at him.

'Hello,' he said again, and the woman stood up and he knew at once that she was Mary Bella.

'Good heavens!' she greeted him, and two of the older men stood up too, and he knew then who they were. They nodded at him and he shook hands with them.

'You've come to lunch!' Mary Bella was amused in a way he had not forgotten, her sudden laughter seeming to brim over as it enlivened her features. Once long, sometimes plaited, her hair was tidily drawn back.

'How are you, sir?' One of the men who'd stood up pulled out a chair for him.

'It's shank of lamb,' Mary Bella said, spooning some on to a plate.

The men finished their food. There was more talk from the older two, reminiscing about the past they associated with him. Then they shook hands again and all the men went off together.

'Gosh,' Mary Bella said, gazing at Anthony in a way he remembered also.

* * *

Driving back to London, Anthony didn't wonder why he'd stayed so long. 'Walk with me a little,' Mary Bella had begged, and it felt natural that he should, that they should walk where they had before, that she should take him to the schoolroom, that he should stay for hours when he hadn't intended to.

He had heard about her mother's death, her father's

so soon afterwards. It was the fate of an only child, Mary Bella had said, to inherit what couldn't be refused. She wasn't complaining. There was nothing of that in her voice, and she'd smiled when she said it, as if it were a comedy that she should own everything because there was no one else. Her smile had come often, as it used to. Her laughter too.

'I wondered,' she had said, 'if ever you would come back.'

She had made tea for them and the flowery china was the same, the cake the one her mother had most often made. He said he had become a cartographer.

A man who hadn't been in the kitchen earlier came in, and Anthony had recognized the lean, baffled features of the man waiting on the ill-lit station platform the night the train was so very late.

'I saw the car,' Woods remarked in bewildered tones that hadn't changed. 'I said to myself whose was it?'

Tired of the motorway he was on, Anthony drove off it. Near Melton Mowbray he stopped in a village and had a drink in the bar of a hotel. After another he didn't want to drive on and spent the night there. He dreamt of the schoolroom as it still was, its windows wedged to keep them from rattling, specks of soot on the unlit kindling in the grate. *Willows whiten, aspens quiver*, Mary Bella recited for him, *Little breezes dusk and shiver*. Once he had been woken in the night by her father, who needed help delivering a calf, and afterwards they had sat drinking whisky until dawn. Unopened letters were always scattered on the table in the hall. Inaccurate clocks were everywhere.

In the morning Anthony knew he shouldn't have gone back.

* * *

A letter came, his handwriting on the envelope. She propped it up on the dresser, to be read when she was alone. 'I never thought of you as patient,' she had confessed the day he came back, 'but of course you must have been.'

She remembered his saying once that patience was worthwhile, and while she waited until the evening, his letter still where she had left it, she thought that that was probably true. *How very strange, seeing you again*, she read at last. *I passed the house by, thinking that time should perhaps be left where it had settled. But I wouldn't have forgiven myself if I hadn't changed my mind.*

She had been kind, the letter said. *Your family's hospitality is all it ever was.* She wondered where he lived. He hadn't told her, and the letter had only London as an address. He'd married someone. She could tell, although he hadn't said that either. She wondered if there were children.

The letter was precious and she folded it again into

the folds he'd made and put it away. It didn't matter that she couldn't reply. He had come back.

* * *

Anthony hadn't made it happen. It had happened because it was part of something else, of what had been impossible and now was not. He told himself that, but it made no difference. He tried to push it all away, but he found he couldn't. Too much was there already, too much had coloured too many moments since they had walked again on the moors, since in the kitchen afterwards she had made tea, since in their schoolroom he had wanted her.

The moors were vast, he reminded himself. He could go back and walk alone there, seeing from afar the house, the farm, and now and again a lonely rider. There could be that.

But when Anthony returned he went at once to the house, and after that he always did.

* * *

Nicola lived with her bewilderment, aware that it wasn't much to have to live with. Yet each morning when she woke she felt uneasy, and didn't want to think. And in the daytime on her own – cleaning, cooking, in a shop – she searched for the calm that had always been hers to call upon, but could not find it. She tried to believe that what she dreaded was only in what she wondered, but could not. Disquiet did not recede, and still the dread was there.

*   *   *

A long flat stone marked Grattan's Tomb. Half fallen, crooked on what was once a hillock and now hardly higher than the surrounding turf, it bore no inscription. Myth claimed this grave, made of its unknown dead an ill-met presence, fearsome on the moors, lone and mad, a chieftain of his ancient times.

'How the past holds on,' Anthony remarked, and Mary Bella knew he was not referring to what an unlettered stone had inspired, but to the past that was theirs. Often their thoughts touched before words expressed them. Someone else, not he, had lived his other life: that fantasy, in silence, was shared.

The August sky was pale, without a cloud, the day as lovely as any Mary Bella had known. The grass around the grave was grazed to a springy shortness, a single clump of cranesbill grown up again from what the sheep had left behind. 'How good this summer is too,' Mary Bella said. 'How good that you have come again today.'

Idyll, he had written for her once and she had loved the word, and more than ever loved it now. *A happiness*, he had written too. Since he'd come back they had not said, and did not say it now, that they would be together in the house. They knew they would be.

Because the house, the moors, were where together they belonged.

* * *

In the dead time of a Sunday afternoon Anthony told the wife he had once loved that their marriage, unchanged for her, had become for him a mistake. He told her gently, in the garden, choosing this time to do so, since their children were with their grandmother and would not be back for more than another hour. The deckchairs they were sitting in were close together because the garden's paved area was restricted.

'It is a shock,' he said. 'I know it is.' He held a hand out and she took it, seeming not quite to realize what she was doing.

Autumn had come, its sunshine a compensation after a disappointing summer. The leaves of shrubs were not yet withering, were only lank, less green. Quite soon the dusk of evening would be there in the afternoon, Nicola had earlier that day remarked.

Her book was open on her knees and she searched for the bookmark she had dropped, then slipped it into place. She had said nothing in response to Anthony's revelation and she didn't now. He watched her walking among their small flowerbeds, picking here and there a weed, gazing down at Michaelmas daisies that yesterday hadn't been in bloom. When she returned to the deckchairs she said that she had known. Her hope that she was wrong was a pretence: she'd known she should not hope.

'Don't say more now,' she begged. 'Please. Not yet.'

She wound around a finger a blade of couch grass she'd picked. He'd left it too long, Anthony thought. All of it was worse because he'd left it so long.

The couch grass cut her when she was careless with it and she threw it away. She put her finger to her lips and he offered to get something for it. She shook her head.

'I'm sorry,' he said.

She tried to read. 'Don't go,' he had thought she would plead, but she hadn't. She didn't plead in any way at all, nor allow her tears to come. 'I'm sorry, Nicola,' he said again.

She shook her head, not looking up from the page that hadn't been turned, and still wasn't in the silence she had asked for. A car door banged and then their children were there, calling out as they ran into the garden, Amelia nine, Susie five.

* * *

Autumn brought with it the bitter wind that, every autumn, blew across the moors. Sheep huddled close, rivulets and bogland froze. Snow came.

But the idyll that had begun in sunshine was still there, its unhurried days, though briefer now, as much a pleasure. Anthony no longer drove away from Old

Grange to begin a journey that familiarity had made
uninteresting. His books were packed into half-empty
bookcases, his coloured inks and pens arranged to his
liking on the schoolroom table. A map of the old
town of Kishinev – his first commission – was framed
and on a wall, his clothes hung beside Mary Bella's in
the wardrobe that had been hers and now was theirs.

Her life had changed less than his. The wages of
the men still had to be paid every week, their midday
meal cooked, her mother's shortcuts with roasts and
stews remembered. She kept the farm accounts as she
had before. She was responsible and in charge, continuing to make her own contribution to how things
should be, what differences were necessary in a different time. A dishwasher for the lunchtime dishes,
because there were so many, made for a less busy day,
as other contemporary devices did. The Aga was electric now, and it was warm in the house as it never was
before. The dog who had been Mary Bella's companion during her time of solitude was suspicious of
another presence, but it didn't matter. Nothing did,
and the days that so smoothly became weeks, then
months, were unlike any that Anthony or Mary Bella
had experienced before; and both believed that nothing could disturb the contentment of being together.

But as November ended, Mary Bella one morning
at breakfast handed across the table a letter addressed
in blue, clear handwriting. She knew at once, although

she hadn't seen the writing before, that it was his wife's. She watched Anthony reading a single, tidily filled page. He read it twice before he gave it to her. 'Nothing can be done about this,' his only comment was.

The older of his two children was starving herself. No reason for her doing so was given, but Mary Bella could guess and knew that Anthony could too.

They did not talk about the letter that morning, or all day. Anthony took it away and Mary Bella imagined he burnt it when he was lighting the drawing-room fire. She never saw it again.

Its contents could not so easily be eluded. They both knew that, and when the post came the following morning the blue handwriting was there again.

'They have taken her into hospital,' Anthony said when he read it. 'For observation, so they say.'

Mary Bella took the letter from him. It said more than he had quoted, but not much. She gathered up the breakfast dishes. He poured more coffee. He said, 'There's nothing to be observed. Nothing mysterious to be discovered. Nothing that isn't known.'

A child had found the pain of her father's absence too much to bear. Silent at first, she cried all day for several days and then began to starve herself. *They ask that you should be told at once*, the clear round writing recorded.

The day he left his family, Susie had helped him to carry his books to the car, following him every few minutes with another pile from the hall. Amelia didn't speak. She didn't come out of her room. But that would pass, he had told himself.

*   *   *

At the hospital they declared that there was nothing particularly unusual about this variation of a child's reaction to extreme distress. They were optimistic and reassuring, and Anthony's presence brought about a recovery that was maintained, as other recoveries had not been. Eventually, it was he who drove Amelia home again, and he stayed for longer than he'd meant to, sleeping on a downstairs sofa and often in the night going to gaze at the somnolent features of his affectionate daughter. They looked as tired as an old woman's, but whenever he touched her forehead with his lips she opened her eyes and sometimes even smiled. Amelia had been born with difficulty but had never before been difficult herself. He remained for more than a week, during which she made amends for the trouble she had caused. She said she wanted to be a cartographer and Anthony was pleased. He understood and was forgiving. He wasn't angry when he was with her.

But three days after he drove into the yard at Old Grange he learnt that she'd again begun to starve herself.

*   *   *

Mary Bella tried not to dwell on what was happening. It wasn't her place to make suggestions and anyway she could think of none. She felt uncomfortable and lost, belonging in what had come about and yet outside it. Anthony had spoken hardly at all about the family he had deserted, his tone when he did so now impersonal, as if he considered that in the circumstances it should be. Of the wife he was still married to, Mary Bella knew little more than her name and that she wrote letters in blue ink, with a fountain pen, not a ballpoint. There were no photographs of her at Old Grange, none that Mary Bella had seen of the two children who had been born. A house had a few times been mentioned, no more than where it was.

Yet out of so little, images came, and voices spoke. As in the schoolroom once Jeanne d'Arc had ridden into battle, as precious stones had glittered on the great high collar of Elizabeth Tudor, so shadows now were more than shadows. The knife that so cruelly and so often fell, the heads that rolled into a mire of blood, the treachery of plots, through their own drama became reality.

The room that has been his is no one's. Its shelves are empty, its drawers are light, his chair is in a corner. The household is bereft, but the pictures on its walls, the patterns on its carpets, are as they always were, and things on tables are. They take away the child again.

*   *   *

Wind whined and whistled, gusts spluttered. On the moors conversation was lost, began again, was lost again. For warmth Mary Bella wore clothes that were rough and of the farm, the coarseness of the tweed, and shabby corduroy, making more of the delicacy in features that Anthony still often saw as a child's. Knowing Mary Bella twice – her mind, her nature, her laughter, her sadness too – he had twice considered her unique, the second time as lovers do about each other.

But in all this Anthony's instinct was as it always had been: not ever to allow in himself the kind of tribulation that haunted Mary Bella. His way was to suppress, to conceal, to be protected. The cartographer's world he had been drawn to was rational and understandable, beyond imagination's interference. He delighted in its accuracy and precision, and made of it what it wanted him to make, discarding what had no purpose.

'We are here, we are together,' he said while the raw cold nagged. 'We live with consequences. We have to, and we can.'

* * *

Mary Bella wondered if they could. Perfection began when he came back, when he called out and she was there as she had always been, all other love rejected.

And yet that memory brought disquiet now that felt like fear.

The snow that earlier had flecked the landscape fell heavily. In the distance, Worley Edge was obscured and they went no further.

'How well you taught me to imagine,' Mary Bella murmured, the softness of her tone not quite conveying the irony of her observation. But what she said was taken by the wind and she did not repeat it. That something demanded more of her was a silent echo on the long walk back, an intimation that would not declare itself yet still was there.

The yard was quiet when they reached it, the men already gone home. The empty house was warm, the blind dog waiting.

*   *   *

The snow fell for days, was blown into drifts, accumulated on the roofs of sheds, on windowsills and frozen panes, changed the shape of water-butts and mounting blocks. It was confining, too.

On the schoolroom table Anthony had spread out an unfinished map of street alterations in Dijon, four paperweights holding it in place, his inks and pens in orderly rows beside it. The table had been put to other uses since he and Mary Bella had shared it in the past – seed potatoes had sprouted on it, apples kept from touching one another, brass and silver polished, china and porcelain repaired. This morning it was shared again, Mary Bella going through the farm accounts at the other end of it.

She would make curtains for the curtainless windows, she had a moment ago decided. And the daisy wallpaper, stained and badly faded by the sun, could be renewed. The white paint of the skirting board and the picture rail could be too, and the paintwork of the door and the window-frames. Their room they called it, and always would.

'All right?' she heard Anthony ask. Then he looked up and smiled at her before he returned to what he'd been doing.

Often she dreamt of the household she could not prevent herself from imagining. And often she lay awake, telling herself that he was right, that people lived with what happened to them, that people had to. Marriages fell apart, he said; it was not unusual. His child was a sensible child, he said; she would be again. One day they would be glad they had held on.

But at night, while Anthony slept, confusion crept into the empty dark, became a tiredness, and Mary Bella heard her own slight whisper speaking of a child who had been damaged, a damaged woman too. She remembered pity from long ago, when in an accident one of the workmen had lost an arm. She had pitied her mother in pain, and a girl at Evelynscourt who was despised, and the blind spaniel who followed her about the house. Challenging the love that kept her silent, her pity now seemed presumptuous when it came in the night, not belonging in an expected way as it had before. Yet still she pitied.

'Yes, I'm all right,' she said, and smiled a little too. In a dream, occurring often, his child was dead and he stood by the grave, alone, flowers spread on the clay. And she watched, hidden by trees, not wanting to be parted from him.

*　*　*

'You are unhappy,' Anthony said one evening in the kitchen when they had finished supper.

Carrying plates and dishes to the sink Mary Bella shook her head but did not answer. Not turning round, she scoured a saucepan she had left on the draining board to steep.

Anthony waited, then dried the dishes he was handed one by one warm from the steaming water. At peace, the old dog slept in his corner.

'Amelia is herself again,' Anthony said. 'You do know that?'

'Yes, I do know.'

'What is it, Mary Bella?'

'A silliness.'

She had told herself this moment would come, yet had believed it might not, that the invasion of her thoughts, no matter how persistent, would slip away, each day, each night, becoming less troubled than the one before.

'It's over now,' Anthony said. 'The awfulness of that time.'

It wasn't over. Since memory would not allow it to be over, it never would be. The damaged do not politely go away, instead release their demons. That must be so, she could not think that it was different.

Soothing and patient, his voice went on. His smile was tender. She loved his pale blue eyes, his hands, his lips, the way he stood, and moved, his quiet laughter. But still his words were nothing. He did not understand.

She tried to say that what had been a wisp of doubt flourished now as premonition, but thought became confusion, did not connect, would not communicate. They could not change themselves, only simulate what was not so.

With that simplicity a loneliness began for Mary Bella that was more than loneliness had ever been before. Belittling the solitude she had so often known, it was mysterious too, coming as it did while she still had the companionship she valued more than any other. 'It's foolishness, all this,' Anthony said.

There was no anger in his tone, no edge of irritation. But both would come when patience had worn itself out. There'd be indifference then, disdain, contempt.

Why did she know? Why did he not? He'd been the teacher once.

*   *   *

The night was slow. Its slowness was their hope, the dawdling hands of the clock on the windowsill their chance to settle what had been disturbed. Time was their genius, Anthony had said: emptily passing, it had held their love before it made of it a high romance.

'We're happy, surely?' He pressed his presumption just a little. 'Shouldn't we be sensible, too?'

But the disturbance that had come did not give up its ground.

*   *   *

The men called out to one another in the yard, early-morning energy in their voices. The herd was driven from the fields for milking. Buckets rattled. Softly a transistor played. In the kitchen, through ragged tiredness, conversation stumbled on.

'How slightly we know ourselves until something happens.' Mary Bella broke a silence that had lasted. 'How blurred the edges are: what we can do, what in the end we can't. What nags, what doesn't.'

Anthony stroked her hair and held her, wanting to for ever. 'Your courage is extraordinary,' he said.

*   *   *

One of the men came in with the morning milk and eggs. Anthony took the milk can from him and filled two blue-and-white kitchen jugs, pouring what remained into a saucepan for their coffee. 'A better day?' he asked and the man said it was brighter than recent days had been. Mary Bella cut bread for toast.

* * *

When spring was about to come and then did not, one morning Anthony wasn't there. Waking early, Mary Bella heard the car.

The men knew more. They'd seen his belongings carried from the house. He'd said goodbye, had shaken their hands. They waved when he drove off, then watched the car becoming nothing on the distant moors.

His clothes, his inks, his pens, unfinished Dijon, his books: all these were gone. Only the old town of Kishinev remained, as he intended it should, a part of him still there.

* * *

She knows his journey, where he will stop, where once he spent a night but has not since and will not now.

She slices gammon, two slices for each plate; the men in turn come for their food. The sun has reached the kitchen, as at this time in spring and summer it always does. Sometimes in the schoolroom he drew the curtains. It will be dusk when he arrives.

She takes her own plate to the table and is deferred to there. In kindness, because kindness is his way, he'll call upon prevarication and deceit, his lies of mercy all he can offer the wife he now returns to. He'll make of love a wild infatuation that did not last and now is over.

The talk at the table is as it always is, about the morning's work, some of it finished, some not yet, about the weather, the forecast for tomorrow. Mary Bella plays a part, for she is used to that. He will be tired, but even so he'll manage, for that too is his way. His grateful wife will not reject him, the broken pieces of what is shattered will be gathered.

The altered fencing of a field is now complete, new gates put in, so she is told, a stile that wasn't there before. He will not come back, not once, not ever. There'll be no tawdry attempt at a revival, no searching in the falsity for something that might be better than nothing.

The men push back their chairs, the shuffling of their boots noisy on the red-tiled floor. Mary Bella senses an anxiety, and pity perhaps. She doesn't try to smile any of that away, only wishes the men could know that love, unchanged, is as it was, is there for him among her shadows, for her in rooms and places as familiar to him as they are to her. She wishes they could know it will not wither, that there'll be no long slow dying, or love made ordinary.

The Women

Cecilia Normanton knew her father well, her mother not at all. Mr Normanton was handsome and tall, with steely grey hair brushed carefully every day so that it was as he wished it to be. His shirts and suits gave the impression of being part of him, as his house in Buckingham Street did, and the family business that bore his name did. Only Mr Normanton's profound melancholy was entirely his own. It was said by people who knew him well that melancholy had not always been his governing possession, that once he had been carefree and a little wild, that the loss of his wife – not to the cruelty of an early death but to her preference for another man – had left him wounded in a way that was irreparable.

Remembered by those who had known it, the marriage was said to have echoed with laughter, that there'd been parties and the pleasure of spending money, that the Normantons had appeared to delight in one another. Yet less than two years after the marriage began it was over; and growing up in the Buckingham Street house, Cecilia heard nothing that was different. 'Your mother isn't here any more,' her father said, and Cecilia didn't know if this was his way of telling her that her mother had died, and didn't feel she could ask. She lived with the uncertainty, but increasingly believed there had been a death from which her father had never recovered and could not speak of. In a pocket-sized yellow folder at the back of a drawer there were photographs of a smiling girl, petite and beautiful, on a seashore and in a garden, and waving from a train. Cecilia's father, smiling too, was sometimes there and Cecilia imagined their happiness, their escapades, their pleasure in being together. She pitied her father as he was now, his memories darkened by his loss

Dark-haired and tall for her age, her legs elegant in schoolgirl black, Cecilia was taken to be older than she was. Eighteen or nineteen was the guess of the youths and men who could not resist a second glance at her prettiness on the street; she was fourteen. She didn't know why she was looked at on the street, for an awareness of being pretty was not yet part of her. It wasn't something that was mentioned by her father or by Mr Grace, the retired schoolmaster whom her father had engaged as her tutor in preference to sending her to one of the nearby schools. It wasn't mentioned by the Maltraverses, who daily came to the house also, to cook and clean.

Among these adult people Cecilia was lonely, and friendless too, in Buckingham Street. At weekends her father did his best, making an effort to be interesting on their strolls about the deserted City streets – the Strand and Ludgate Hill, Cheapside and Poultry, Threadneedle Street, Cornhill. He pointed out the Bank of England, the Stock Exchange: a village in its way, he said, London's City was. Sometimes, as a change, he booked two rooms at a small hotel in Suffolk, usually at Hintlesham or Orford.

Cecilia enjoyed these weekend excursions, but the weekdays continued to pass slowly, for Mr Grace came only in the mornings and the Maltraverses were not given to conversation. In the afternoons, when she had completed the work she'd been set, she had the spacious rooms of the house to herself and poked about in drawers, watched television, or opened the yellow folder to look again at the photographs of her mother. When she had money she went out to buy liquorice allsorts or a Kit Kat.

She was fortunate, she knew. No one was unkind to her, no one was angry. She imagined nothing would change, that Mr Grace would always come, the Maltraverses always be too busy for conversation, that always there'd be the silent afternoon house, the drawers, and being alone. But sensitive to the pressure of duty where his child was concerned, her father did not demur when he was advised that the time had come to send her away to boarding school, to be a girl among other girls.

* * *

'You shall have a flowerbed,' Miss Watson said.

Smart as a mannequin, she was delicately attractive in different ways. Her voice, her slimness, the gentleness in her eyes. A softly woven scarf – a galaxy of reds and rust against the grey of her dress – was loosely draped and almost reached the ground.

'We are happy people here,' she assured Cecilia. 'You shall be too.'

Amhurst, the school was called, and Miss Watson, who was its headmistress, explained how the name had come about, told how the school had been the seat of a landed family, how outbuildings had been transformed into music rooms and laboratories, art rooms and the weaving room, only the classroom blocks being a new addition. She took Cecilia to a small brick-walled garden which was, and always had been, the headmistress's. She opened an ornamental iron gate in an archway, then latched it again as if shutting away everything of the school itself. She pointed at a flowerbed with nothing growing in it and said it would be Cecilia's, where she could cultivate the flowers she liked best. Old Trigol was the school gardener, she said, a dear person when you got to know him.

Cecilia disliked the place intensely, felt lonelier and more on her own than she ever had in Buckingham Street. She wrote to her father, begging him to come and take her away. She was the only new girl that term and no one bothered with her except a senior girl whom Miss Watson had ordered to. 'You pray?' this older girl asked her, and suggested that they might pray together. *Every meal's inedible*, Mr Normanton read. *A girl was sick after pilchards.*

But as time went on Cecilia's letters became less wretched. She discovered Mozart, Le Douanier Rousseau and, recommended by the religious girl, St Theresa of Lisieux. She read *The Moon and Sixpence* and then *The Constant Nymph*. Two girls, called Daisy and Amanda, became her friends. The religious girl reported to Miss Watson that settling in had begun.

Mr Normanton came often during that first term. He took Cecilia out on weekend exeats – lunch at the Castletower Hotel, tea in the tearooms on the river. He met Daisy and Amanda, and before the term ended took them out too. He was glad he had listened to the advice he'd been given, had realized what he hadn't on his own: that his child would benefit and be happy as a girl among other girls.

Cecilia grew lily of the valley in her flowerbed, having decided it was her favourite flower. She picked the first bunch on her fifteenth birthday and offered it to Miss Watson.

'You are a person we take pride in, Cecilia,' Miss Watson said.

*   *   *

The two women who were watching the hockey were on the other touchline, directly opposite where Cecilia, with Daisy and Amanda, was watching it too, since attendance at all home matches was compulsory. Cecilia remembered the women being on the touchline before because when the hockey had ended they'd passed close to where she and Daisy and Amanda were looking for Amanda's watch, which had slipped from her wrist without her noticing. 'Someone'll stand on it!' Amanda was wailing, and the two women had hesitated as if about to look for the watch too. Daisy found it, undamaged on the grass, and the women went on. But when they had hesitated they had stared at Cecilia in a way that was disconcerting.

There was sudden cheering and clapping: Amhurst had scored. St Hilda's – in their unbecoming brown jerseys a glum contrast to Amhurst's jolly red-and-blue – looked defeated already and probably would be, for Amhurst never lost. It would have been Elizabeth Statham who'd scored, Cecilia imagined, and hoped it wasn't or it would mean a lot of showing off later on. But Amanda said it was. 'Bloody Statham,' Daisy muttered.

They wanted St Hilda's to win. Favouring the other

side eased their indignation at having to stand in the cold for an hour and a half on a winter's afternoon: they hated watching hockey almost more than anything.

'I tried to read *Virginibus Puerisque*,' Amanda said. 'Ghastly.'

Daisy agreed, and recommended *Why Don't They Ask Evans?*. Cecilia wondered who the women who'd come back only a few weeks after they'd been before were. They wouldn't be Old Girls because Old Girls always hung around Miss Watson or Miss Smith and they weren't doing that. They wouldn't be supporters of St Hilda's because the visiting team hadn't been St Hilda's the other time. She wondered if for some reason they enjoyed watching hockey matches, as Colonel Forbes enjoyed watching cricket and always came, Saturday after Saturday, in the summer term. Trigol was allowed to take the afternoon off from the garden for Sports Day because he'd once been a high-jump champion, which wasn't easy to imagine, Trigol being in his seventies now.

When the two women had stared at Cecilia, the smaller one had smiled. Cecilia had smiled back since it would have been rude not to, but Daisy and Amanda hadn't seen that any more than they'd seen the staring, and afterwards Cecilia had said nothing because it was embarrassing, and silly to go on about.

Miss Chalmers blew the final whistle and there were three cheers for St Hilda's and then for Amhurst, followed by clapping when the two teams walked off the pitch. The people who'd been watching followed, groups breaking up and new ones forming as they made their way back to the school buildings. The two women became lost in the crowd and Cecilia was aware of feeling relieved. But they were there again, by the cattle grid, where cars were parked on match days. The St Hilda's coach was there too, the driver folding away the newspaper he'd been reading. The two women didn't get into a car and drive off, as Cecilia thought they would. They stood about as if they had a reason to, and Cecilia avoided looking in their direction.

* * *

They had taken the path through the trees and, emerging from what had become a small wood, they marvelled at the open land, as earlier they had marvelled at sunshine in February, misty though it was. Nothing as tiresome as rain had spoilt their walk from the railway station, or their returning to it now.

'I would have travelled a million miles for this afternoon,' Miss Keble summed up their outing as they approached the first of the bungalows on the town's outskirts.

Miss Cotell – less given to exaggeration than her friend – said nothing, but in her reticence there was no denial that the afternoon had been a pleasure. How could it not have been, she thought, their presence for the second time unquestioned, and the feeling as well that they had been right to return? How could all that not have been a treat?

Miss Keble, sensing these thoughts, kept the subject going, marvelling that so little achieved should seem so much of a triumph, yet understanding that it should be. She would not easily forget the faces of the girls, their voices too, and how politely they'd stood back, respecting strangers. All of it was impossible to forget.

Miss Cotell again was silent but still no less impressed and then, quite suddenly, as affected in a different way, an urge to weep restrained. On the train her tears, permitted now, were not of sorrowing nor distress but came because her friend understood so much so well, because agreement between them, never faltering, had been today more than it had ever been before.

Guessing all this, Miss Keble watched Miss Cotell recover her composure. For some minutes they both gazed out at landscape that wasn't impressive until, cut into the limestone of a distant hill, there was an image of a prehistoric animal.

'I'm sorry,' Miss Cotell apologized. 'Stupid.'

'Of course it wasn't.'

Miss Keble went in search of tea, but there wasn't any to be found. Miss Cotell fell asleep.

The two – of an age at fifty-eight – had retired early from a government department. They had first met there thirty-odd years ago and their friendship had flourished on the mores of office life, Miss Keble remaining in Benefits (Family), Miss Cotell making a brief foray into Pensions and then returning to Benefits. They had been together since, as close in retirement as they were before it.

The landscape Miss Cotell was unaware of while she dreamt instantly forgotten dreams faded into winter dusk. Miss Keble failed to interest herself in a newspaper someone else had left behind and instead thought about the house they were returning to, about the rooms in which their two lives had become entangled over the years, for which furniture, piece by piece, had been chosen together, where childhood memories had been exchanged. Miss Keble, as she sometimes did when she was away from the house for longer than usual, saw in a vision the reminders it held of foreign places where there'd been holidays: the Costa del Sol, the beach at Rimini, Vernon, where they'd stayed when they'd visited Monet's garden, the unidentified setting where an obliging stranger had operated Miss Cotell's Kodak, allowing them to pose together. The house, the rooms, these images of themselves in the places where they'd been meant everything to Miss Keble, as equally they did to Miss Cotell.

The house, in a terrace, was small, without a garden. At the back, the feature of a concrete yard was a row of potted plants arranged against a cream-distempered wall. Curtains of fine net protected the two downstairs front windows from the glances of passing pedestrians; at night, flowery chintz was drawn across; upstairs there were blinds. Everything – and in the yard too – had been made as Miss Cotell and Miss Keble wanted it, an understanding that became another element in their relationship. Nothing had been undertaken, no changes made, without agreement.

This house, in darkness, became theirs again when their train journey ended. It was cold and they switched on electric fires. They discussed what food should be cooked, or not cooked, if tonight they should open a tin of salmon or manage on sandwiches and tea. Both settled for a poached egg on toast.

'It was good of you, Keble,' Miss Cotell said when, snug in their heated kitchen, they sat down to eat. 'I have to thank you.'

Their calling one another by surname only was a habit left behind by office life, for although they did not regret their early retirement, office life clung on. They had wondered about other clerkly work, but it wasn't easy – and in the end impossible – to find anything suitable, especially since they stipulated that they should not be separated.

'Both times I wanted to come with you,' Miss Keble said. 'And I will again.'

Tidily, Miss Cotell drew her knife and fork together on her empty plate. 'I wonder, though,' she said, 'if I have the heart for going there again.'

'Oh, what a thing, Cotell! Of course you have!'

'What more can come of it?' And whispering, as if she spoke privately, although there was no privacy between them, Miss Cotell softly repeated, 'What more?'

Miss Keble knew and did not say. Warm and pleasant, the euphoria brought about by the day still possessed her, more ordinarily than it did her friend. She wished Miss Cotell no ill will, wished her all the peace in the world, but still could not help welcoming in a way that was natural to her the exhilaration she experienced. She did not press or urge: they were neither of them like that. Resisting the flicker of satisfaction that threatened to disturb her features, she gathered up the cups and saucers.

Miss Cotell folded the tablecloth and put away the salt and pepper. 'How difficult,' she murmured, 'to know what's right.'

'Of course,' Miss Keble said.

* * *

It wasn't until the following term that Cecilia again saw the two women. Summer had come, the long, light evenings, the smell of grass just cut, the flower-beds of Miss Watson's brick-walled garden bright with crocosmia and sweet pea, with echium and sanguineum. When she was younger, Cecilia had preferred the cosiness of winter, but no longer did. She loved the sunshine and its warmth, her too-pale skin lightly browned, freckles on her arms.

She saw the women when she was returning from taking the afternoon letters to the post-box, a fourth-form duty that came on a rota once a fortnight. She had called into Ridley's when the letters were posted – honeycomb chocolate for Daisy, Mademoiselle's bonbons. The women were on the path through the trees, coming towards her.

They must live nearby, Cecilia thought. Probably they went for walks and had found their way to the hockey pitch. But hockey was over now until September.

Sunlight came through the trees in shafts, new beech leaves making dappled shadows on the women's clothes. How drab those clothes were, Cecilia thought. How ugly the taller woman's features were, the hollow cheeks, her crooked teeth, one with a corner gone. Her friend was dumpy.

They had stopped and Cecilia felt she should also, although she didn't want to.

'What weather at last!' the dumpy woman said.

They asked her her name and said that was a lovely

name when she told them. Violets were held out to her to smell. They said where they'd picked them. A dell they called the place, near the fingerpost. They could have picked an armful.

'We hoped we'd see you,' the taller woman said. 'For you, my dear.'

Again the violets were held out, this time for Cecilia to take.

'We're not meant to pick the flowers.'

Both smiled at once. 'You didn't pick them, you might explain. A gift.'

'Look this way, Cecilia,' the dumpy woman begged.

She had a camera, but the distant chiming of the afternoon roll-call bell had already begun, and Cecilia said she had to go.

'Just quickly, dear.' They both spoke at once, saying they mustn't keep her, and when she hurried away Cecilia heard the voices continuing, a monotone kept low, hardly changing from one voice to the other. She could tell she was being watched, that the women were standing there instead of going on.

'Who are they?' Elizabeth Statham was in her running clothes, returning from the afternoon run she went on to keep in training for the games she was so good at. 'Friends of yours?' she asked.

'I don't know them at all.'

'Funny they'd take a photograph.'

Cecilia didn't attempt to reply. Frightened of

Elizabeth Statham, she was at her worst with her, never knowing what to say.

'Funny they'd want to give you flowers.'

Cecilia tried to shrug, but her effort felt clumsy and Elizabeth Statham sniggered.

'Poor relations, are they?'

'I don't know them.'

She couldn't hear the women any more, and imagined they must have gone. She didn't look back. Elizabeth Statham would go on about it because she had a way of doing that, sitting on your bed after lights out, pretending to be nice.

'Funny they'd know your name,' she said before she continued on her run.

*   *   *

'Come now,' Miss Keble said that same evening, when they were home again and it was late.

Miss Cotell, not at first responding, said when the pause had become drawn out, 'A dullness settles on me when I try to think. "I'll think it through," I tell myself, and then I can't. That dullness comes, as if I've summoned it.'

'It's called being in two minds.' Miss Keble, sprightly, gave her opinion.

'I feel I have no mind at all.'

'Oh, now!' Miss Keble smiled and firmly shook her head.

'How good you are to me, Keble,' Miss Cotell thanked her friend before she went upstairs.

Miss Keble did not deny it.

*   *   *

Miss Cotell undressed and for a moment before she reached for her nightdress stood still, her nakedness reflected in her looking-glass. How old she seemed, the flesh of her neck all loops and furrows, her arms gone scrawny. The hair that Broughton had called her crowning glory was greyer and thinner than it should have been: she blamed herself, but blaming didn't help. 'How could I!' she had protested, laughing almost when Broughton had asked if she would show herself to him.

'Please,' he begged. 'Please.' He wouldn't now. He'd held her to him, the buttons of his jacket cold.

Shy as a bird she'd heard him called, but oh, he wasn't. With her he could not be, he'd said.

Slowly Miss Cotell drew on her nightdress, then felt the sheets, the pillow, cold. He'd warmed her, and tonight she had known he would again. The caressing of his murmur did, and his touch was more than she could bear, his hands so soft as if all his life he had done no physical work. The blue of his eyes was a paler blue than she'd ever seen in eyes before, his hair like down, wheat-coloured, lovely. He whispered now as he had then and she did too, in the dark, since always they wanted that. She dried his tears of shame. She loved his body's warmth. He'd chosen her. She'd wanted no one else.

* * *

Miss Keble, who had not experienced this aspect of life, was aware without resentment that she lived at second-hand. Her friend had done things: their reminiscences, so often exchanged, allowed no doubt about that. Yet Miss Cotell, seeming to lead the way, did not. Miss Keble, through listening and knowing what should be done, had years ago taken charge. 'How little I would be, alone,' Miss Cotell had a way of saying, and Miss Keble loved to hear it. Accepting her lesser role, she knew that it was she, in the end, who ordered their lives and wielded power.

She turned the pages of an old book she had never thrown away and knew almost by heart, *Dr Bradley Remembers*. But her thoughts did not connect with the people it again presented to her. What innocence there was in the girl's eyes! She closed her own and saw the unspoilt features still a child's, the dark, dark hair, the blue-and-red blazer, the pleated grey skirt. Vividly, recollection refreshed for Miss Keble all that the day had offered, and the joy that should have been her friend's became her own.

* * *

Miss Cotell dreamt. When she answered the doorbell Father Humphrey was standing there, his back to her at first. 'All done,' he said, his voice stern, his handshake firm.

'Thank you,' he said, not opening the envelope she gave him.

*   *   *

Because Cecilia was to be Thisbe, Mr Normanton was given a seat in the front row. His daughter's ambition, he knew, was one day to be an actress, a secret shared only with him. There had been such intimacies since Cecilia had gone away to Amhurst, as if each separation and each pleasurable reunion had influenced a closeness that had not been evident, or felt, before. He understood Cecilia's reluctance to reveal to her friends the presumption of a talent, to keep from them her English teacher's prediction that she would in time play Ophelia, and one day Lady Macbeth. It delighted Mr Normanton that all this had come about, that his solitary child had been drawn out in ways he had not been able to find himself, that in spite of his awkwardness as a father she had turned to him with her confidences.

Miss Watson took her place beside him, whispering something he couldn't hear. The house lights dimmed, all chatter ceased.

*   *   *

Miss Cotell and Miss Keble talked about the evening, tickets for which Miss Keble had discovered could be purchased by the public when the requirements of friends and parents had been satisfied. They'd been at the back and more than a little cramped but hadn't minded. They had noticed the honouring of Mr Normanton, placed next to the headmistress, and when someone asked Miss Keble who he was she was able to say he was the father of the girl who had been enthusiastically applauded as Thisbe.

It was almost midnight now and in their bed-and-breakfast room their beds were close enough to allow for conversation that would not disturb if their voices were kept low. Tonight had felt like the height of what they could hope for, Miss Cotell reflected, the end at last of what had been a beginning when, alone, she had visited what Father Humphrey called the priest house on a cold April afternoon a long time ago now. 'He'll come to you when he's ready,' a slatternly woman curtly informed her and didn't answer when Miss Cotell remarked on the weather.

'Well, now?' Father Humphrey greeted her when he came, a big, tall man who asked her how she had heard of him and she explained that another girl in Pensions had mentioned him.

Awake, Miss Keble was drawn back to that afternoon too. In hearing about it there had been a description of the slovenly woman, her dishevelled

grey hair hanging in wisps about her face, her fingernails edged with black; and the priests who'd passed
silently through the room while Miss Cotell waited
had been described in similar detail. The two women
had thought it likely that tonight they would talk again
about that time, but found they didn't. A lorry drew
up on the street outside, a door was banged and a
man's voice said, 'This place'll do.' A dog began to
bark but not for long.

Miss Cotell and Miss Keble slept then. Period cos-
tumes coloured their unconsciousness, and the
rhythms of period music were faintly there again; and
Mr Normanton's dark blue suit was, his polka-dotted
tie, the hat he carried with his coat.

'I cannot leave,' Miss Cotell confessed at breakfast.
'I cannot without saying how all of it was wonderful.
I cannot, Keble.'

They bought two gifts, Miss Cotell's a narrow bracelet of coloured stones set in silvered plate, Miss Keble's
a selection of chocolates she was assured were special.
They had become familiar with the bells of the school,
the one that ended classes, the lunchtime summons, the
roll-call bell at half past four, the hurry-up one five minutes later. They knew a clearing in the woods and
brought the sandwiches they made there. They could
see the path, but no one appeared on it all day.

It had to be said, Miss Keble, impatient, told herself
while they waited. It had to be and Cotell was not the

one to say it, for it was not her way. Cotell did not ever press herself, never had, never would. Too easily she went timid. But even so, and more than ever, Miss Keble could see in her friend's eyes the longing that had so often been there since they'd first begun to come here. She could sense it today, in gestures and intimations, in tears blinked back.

At twenty past four they walked to the school.

* * *

Cecilia caught a single glimpse of the two women and looked away and didn't look again. Whoever was on afternoon duty would surely ask them what they wanted, why they were here in Founder's Quad where visitors never were without a reason. She heard a prefect asking who they were, and someone saying she didn't know. It was a relief at least that Elizabeth Statham was excused this roll-call because every afternoon now she had to train for Sports Day.

'We wanted just to say how much we enjoyed last night,' the taller of the women said, and the dumpy one added that wild horses wouldn't have stopped them coming back to say it.

'These are for you,' the tall one said.

They held out packages in different-coloured wrapping paper, and Cecilia remembered the flowers they'd pressed on her, which she'd had to throw away. It was Miss Smith on duty, but she appeared to be

unconcerned by the women's presence, even acknow-
ledging it with a hospitable nod in their direction as
if she remembered them from last night. They spoke
softly to one another when the roll was called and
while Miss Smith read out two brief announcements.

'Cecilia, if you visited us,' the dumpy woman said
then, 'you would like our house. We're not that far
away.' She said that the packages, which Cecilia had
not accepted, were gifts, that the address of their house
was included with them, the phone number too.

No one was near enough to hear and the curiosity
about the two women had dissipated. Already girls
were moving away.

'They are for you,' the tall woman repeated.

Cecilia took the packages, then changed her mind
and put them on a seat. 'I don't know you. It's kind of
you to give me presents but I don't know why you
want to.'

'Cecilia,' the dumpy woman said, 'you'll have heard
of Father Humphrey?'

'I think you're mistaking me for someone else.'

The tall woman shook her head. She had looked
startled when the name was mentioned, had held a
hand out as if protesting that it shouldn't be, anxiety
in her eyes.

'Father Humphrey died,' the other woman went
on, disregarding all this. 'Miss Cotell heard. And
when she went back to the priest house she asked me

to be with her for support. The same housekeeper was there, and I said that any papers left behind might concern Miss Cotell. The housekeeper had her objections but she let us peruse the papers for five minutes only and, truth to tell, five minutes were enough. Father Humphrey was a man who wrote everything down.'

Cecilia wondered if the women were unbalanced, if they had found a way of wandering from a home for the deranged. For a moment she felt sorry for them but then the smaller one began to talk about their house, about a cat called Raggles, and flowers in pots, and after a hesitation the tall one joined in. They didn't sound then as Cecilia imagined the mad would sound, and the moment of pity passed. The cat had strayed into their back yard as a kitten. Their house was called Sans Souci. If she came she could spend a night, they said. They spoke as if they were suggesting she should come often and described the bedroom she would have, which they had wallpapered themselves.

'How much we'd like it if you came!' Through the anxiety that had not gone away, the tall woman smiled as she spoke, her chipped tooth, crooked and discoloured, sticking out more than the others.

'My dear, Miss Cotell is your mother,' Miss Keble said.

* * *

Cecilia went away, leaving the two packages on the seat, but she had gone only a few yards when she heard the women's voices, raised and angry as she never had before. She looked back once and only for a moment.

They were not as she had left them. They confronted one another, trying to keep their voices down but not succeeding. 'I gave my sworn word,' the woman who had been called her mother was bitterly exclaiming.

The voices clashed in accusation and denial, contempt and scorn; and there was the sobbing then of the woman who felt herself deprived. She had wanted only to be near her child, all she deserved. 'No more than that.' Cecilia heard the words choked out. 'And in your awful jealousy how well you have destroyed the little I might have had.'

Cecilia hurried then. 'We cannot come back,' she heard, but only just. 'Not once again. Not ever now.'

There was a protest furiously snapped out, and nothing after that was comprehensible. Cecilia kept trying again to think of the women as unbalanced, and then she tried not to think of them at all. Afterwards she told no one what had been said, not even Daisy and Amanda, who naturally would have been interested.

* * *

That summer Mr Normanton took his daughter to the Île de Porquerolles. In previous summers he had taken her to Cap-Ferrat, to Venice and Bologna, to

Switzerland, making time on each journey for a stay in Paris. It was on these excursions that Cecilia first came to know her father better. More of his life was revealed, more of a past that he'd thought would not interest her. His childhood added a dimension to his lonely father's role; his young man's world did too. Every time Cecilia returned from school to Bucking-ham Street she was aware that melancholy disturbed him less than it had. On their holidays together it was hardly there at all.

At Porquerolles, while every bay of the island's coast, every creek, every place to swim was visited, Cecilia felt her company relished; and her father's quiet presence was a pleasure, which it had not always been. Silences, a straining after words to keep a con-versation going, uncertainty and doubt, too often once had become the edgy feeling that nothing was quite right.

It was hot in August, but a breeze made walking comfortable and they walked a lot. They talked a lot too, Cecilia especially – about her friends at school, the books she had read during the term that had just ended, Elizabeth Statham's subtle bullying. She hadn't meant to say anything about the women who'd been a nuisance and when something slipped out she regret-ted it at once.

'They wanted money?' her father asked, stopping for a moment in their walk along the cliffs to look for a way down to the rocky shore below, and going on when there was none.

'No, not at all,' Cecilia said. 'They were just peculiar women.'

'Sometimes people who approach you like that want money.'

He was dressed as he never was in London, casually, without a jacket, in white summer trousers, a coloured scarf which she had given him at his throat, his shirt collar open. Cecilia, who particularly noticed clothes, liked all this much better than the formality of his suits. She said so now. The women were not mentioned again.

But that evening when his whisky had been brought to him on the terrace of the hotel he said, 'Tell me more about your women.'

Cecilia bit into an olive, cross with herself again. He was curious, and of course bewildered, because she'd left out so much – the women being there at the hockey matches and then appearing on the way through the woods, and how she'd thought they might suffer from a mental affliction. She described their clothes and the way they had of speaking at the same time, each often saying something different, how they related in detail the features of their house and spoke of their cat. Her father listened, nodding and smiling occasionally. She didn't tell him everything.

Shreds of the day's warmth were gaudy in the

evening sky as the terrace slowly filled and new conversations began. A dog obediently lay down beneath
a chair and was no trouble even when the couple with
him finished their drinks and went off to the restaurant without him. A Frenchman, relating an experience
he had recently had, brought it to an end and was
rewarded with quiet laughter. Cecilia, puzzled by *jeu
blanc*, used several times, missed the point.

'I played a lot of tennis once,' her father remarked
when they were being led to their table in the restaurant. 'I doubt I ever told you that.'

'Were you good?'

'No, not at all. But I liked playing. *Jeu blanc*'s a love
game.'

* * *

On their last morning, walking to the harbour as
every day they had during their stay, Cecilia talked
about becoming an actress and heard more than she
had before about her father's work and his office colleagues, about the house in Buckingham Street when
first he knew it, about being married there. Passing
the farm that was the beginning of the village, he
said, 'The marriage fell to pieces. When we tried to
put it together again we couldn't. I let you believe as
you did because it was the easier thing and sometimes,
even, I pretended to myself that it was true. I was
ashamed of being rejected.'

Bougainvillaea hung over garden walls. Across the street from the crowded fruit stall, the café they liked best hadn't come to life yet, their usual table not taken, as often it was. Their coffee was brought before they ordered it.

'I thought that perhaps you guessed,' her father said. 'About the marriage.'

Old men played dominoes in a corner, the waiters stood about. A woman and child came hurrying in. The girl who worked the coffee machine pointed at a door.

'During all your life as I have known it,' Cecilia's father said, 'you have made up for what went wrong in mine.'

*　*　*

On the quays they watched the slow approach of the ferry. There was a stirring in the crowd waiting to embark, luggage gathered up, haversacks swung into place. A ragged line was formed when two ticket collectors arrived. The newcomers who came off the ferry trundled their suitcases to where the grey mini-bus from the hotel was parked.

'We should call in at the Tourist Information,' Cecilia's father said, but when they did they found they didn't have to because the times of the early-morning boats to the mainland – on one of which they hoped to be tomorrow – were listed in the window.

They bought a baguette and thinly sliced ham in the village, and peaches and a newspaper. They had another cup of coffee in the café.

'I'm sorry,' her father said. 'For hating the truth so much, for so long.'

*　*　*

On the walk back to the hotel Cecilia didn't say what she might have said, nor ask what she might have asked. She didn't want to know.

They rested in the shade, beneath dry dusty trees. People on bicycles cycled by and smiled at them and waved. Faintly in the distance they could hear the rattle of the minibus returning to the harbour.

'Shall we go on?' her father suggested, his hands held out to her.

*　*　*

She drew the curtains in her room, darkening the lit-up brightness of the afternoon. She thought she might weep when she lay down, and spread a towel over her pillow in case she did. Fragments made a whole: the photographs that were lies, the marriage that fell apart. No child was born; they'd hoped one would be. As best they could they had made up for that, but what had been was over. Suitcases instead were in the hall, coats and dresses trailing from hangers piled together. A taxi drove away. He watched it go, alone but for a child who, by chance belonging nowhere, now belonged to him.

Maids came to turn the bed down. Cecilia said to leave it and thanked them for the chocolate they had put out for her on her bedside table. She called out, apologizing when her father knocked softly on the door. She had a headache; she would not come down tonight. He didn't fuss. He never did. His footsteps went away.

* * *

The night didn't hurry when it came. She did not want it to. Tomorrow he would finish what he had begun: she had that now. 'I have to tell you this as well,' gently he would say, and ask to be forgiven when he did. She didn't blame him for what he had withheld. She understood; he had explained. But still he would complete what wasn't yet complete because he felt he should.

* * *

They were early at Toulon for their train to Paris and took it in turns to walk about the streets so that their luggage wouldn't be left unattended. Morosely, Cecilia gazed into the shop windows, hardly seeing their contents. Again the women hovered, as in reality they had. Their voices did, their clothes, the clergyman they talked about, their house, their cat. Her father's silence would not hold; he did not want it to. He would tell her on the train.

Or even now, Cecilia thought when they waited together on the platform. In a strange place, among hurrying people, there'd be a moment that seemed right and he would choose his words. He would say again her presence in his house made up for his unhappiness there, and tell her what she had to know.

But when her father spoke it was to praise the train they waited for. An express that haughtily ignored Marseille and Montpellier, Lyon and Dijon too, stopping only twice. 'The best trains in the world,' he said. 'And we can have a *croque* for lunch.'

They had it standing at the counter of the bar and their talk was about the island and how they would always want to return to the little bays, the clear deep water, their daily explorations, the café they had liked. Cecilia's panic receded a little and then a little more; her father's politeness was measured and firm, as if he'd been aware of her brooding and understood it. He drew the conversation out and kept it going. She could read it in his face that he had changed his mind.

Afterwards in an almost empty carriage their seats faced one another, were on their own, and quiet. Her father read *Bleak House*, a book he liked to go back to, and she didn't feel neglected by his absorption in it as on other journeys she sometimes had when he read. His occasional smile of pleasure, his delicate fingers turning the pages, his summer clothes uncreased in spite of travel, reflected the ease with himself that had been slow in becoming what it was. He had borne his bitterness well. Somewhere, today and every day, the wife he had not ceased to love enjoyed the contentment he had been unable to give her. With cruel fortitude he might have allowed himself to dwell on her life without him, but he preferred an emptiness, and made of it something better than the truth.

Cecilia knew it; and emulating his skill in living with distress, allowed his silence to continue because there was nothing else to reveal. The women nurtured in the lonely lives they shared a fantasy that dressed things up a bit. They sought out girls without a mother, befriending them in order themselves to be befriended. There was excitement in the shadowlands of what might have been, in the bluster of daring and pretending, and drama that made a talking point.

This flimsy exercise in assumption and surmise crept, unsummoned, into Cecilia's thoughts and did not go away. Shakily challenging the apparent, the almost certain, its suppositions were vague, inchoate. Yet they were there, and Cecilia reached out for their whisper of consoling doubt.